I0753048

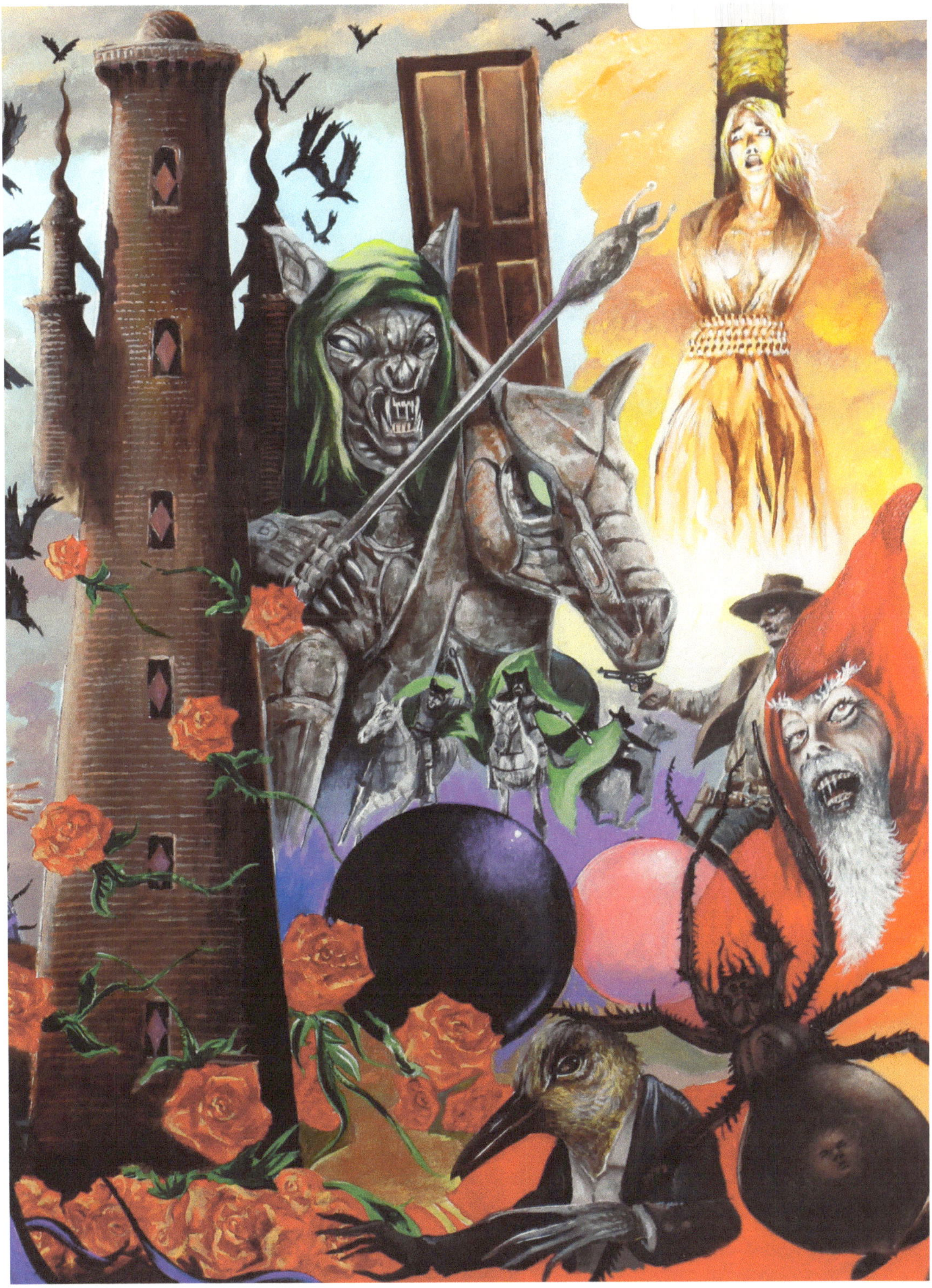

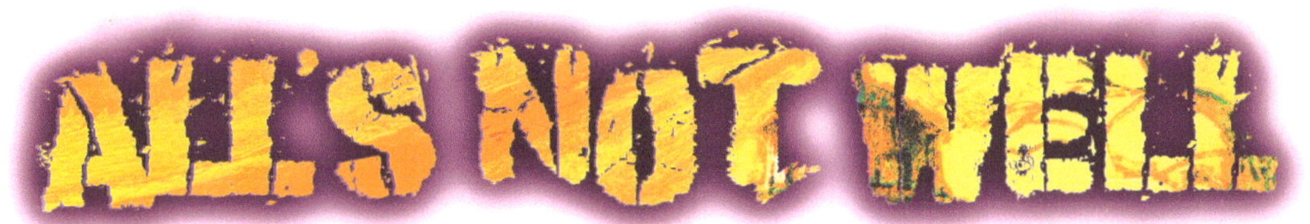

The Gallery of Glenn Chadbourne

A World Horror Convention Sampler

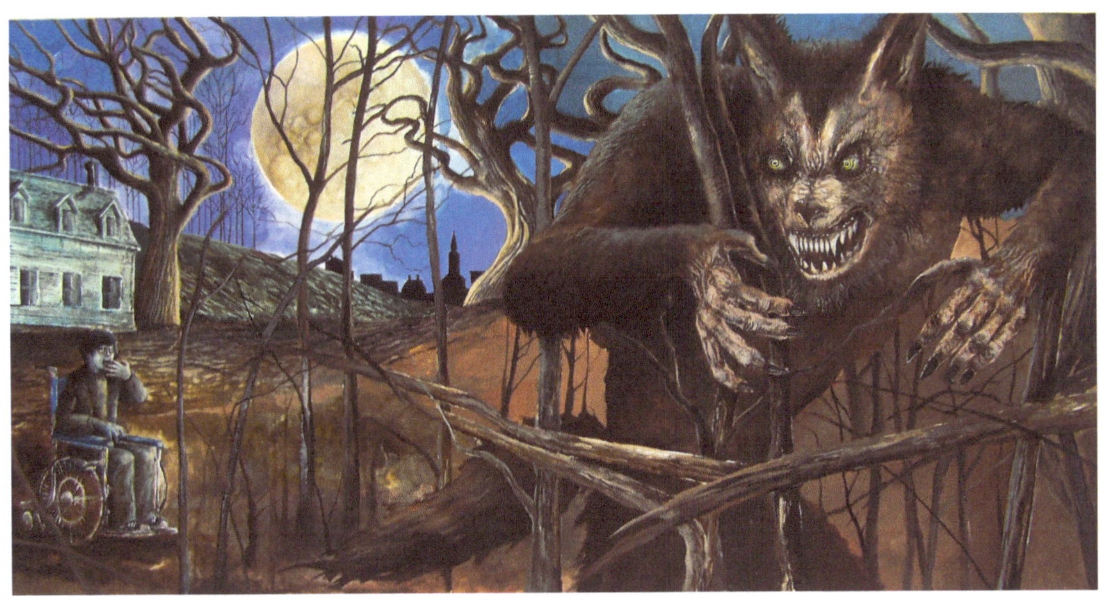

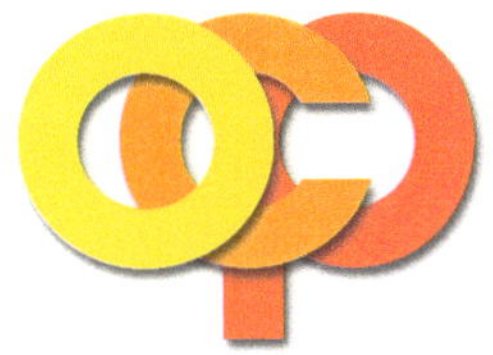

Overlook Connection Press

2013

This edition is published to honor Glenn Chadbourne's Artist Guest of Honor appearance at The 2013 World Horror Convention in New Orleans, Louisiana, June 13th-16th.

Overlook Connection Press
PO Box 1934, Hiram, Georgia 30141
www.overlookconnection.com
overlookcn@aol.com

First Edition
Trade Paperback ISBN: 978-1-62330-031-9

CONTENTS

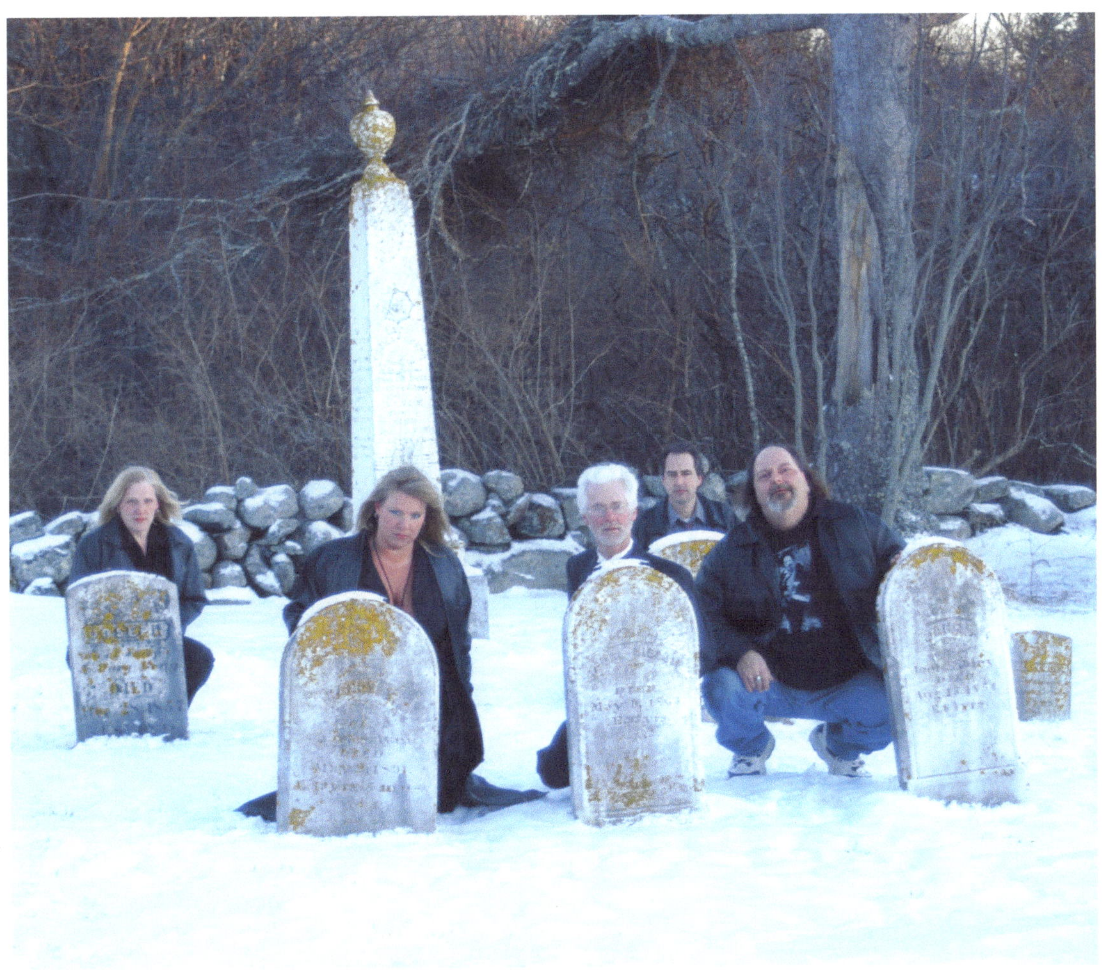

Nick Noxious and the Necrophiliacs

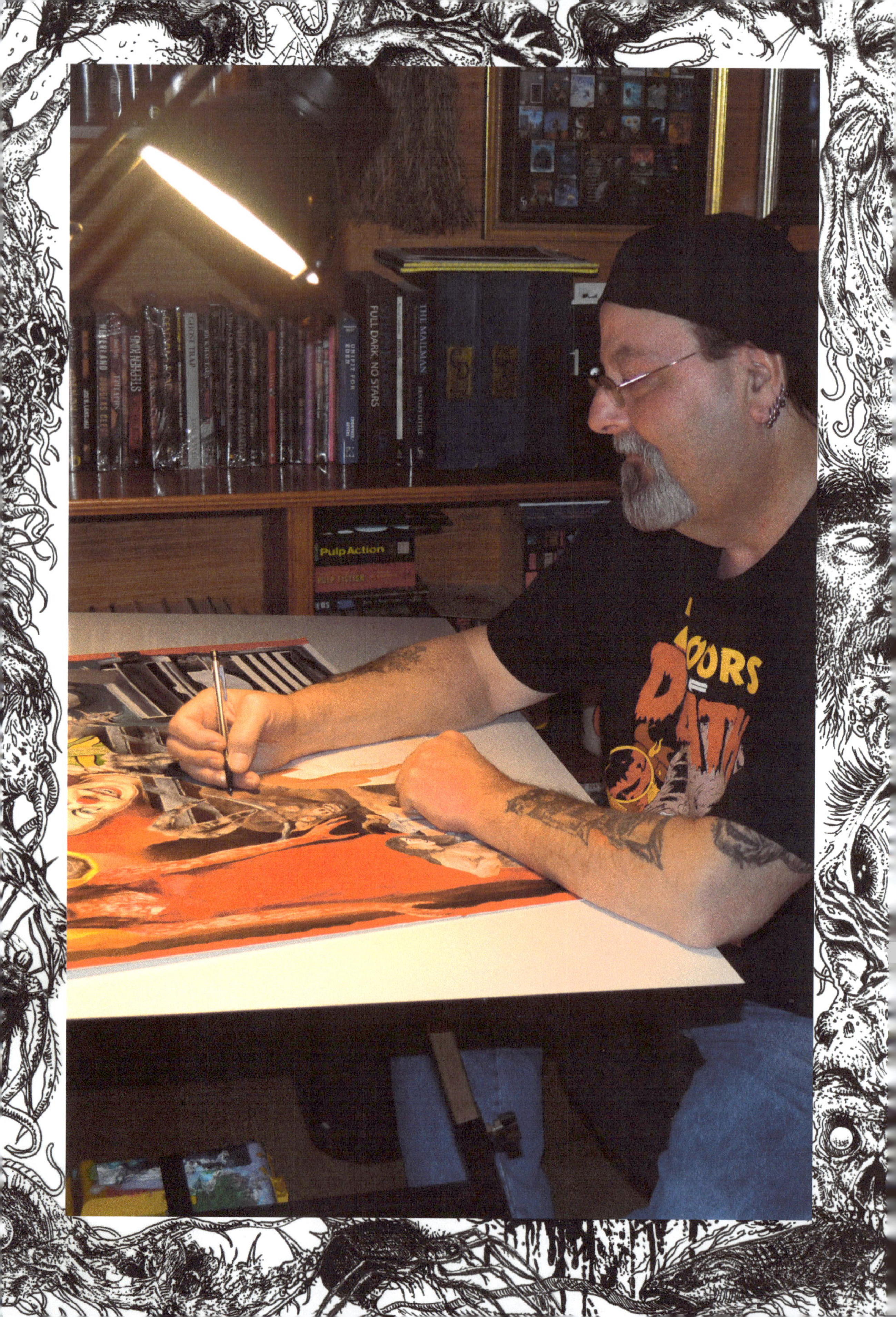
STEPHEN KING
FULL DARK, NO STARS
THE MAILMAN
Pulp Action

The Horror of Chadbourne

By Dave Hinchberger

Sounds like a one of those Hammer flicks, a town of Lovecraftian horror so immersed in its own slime that the title oozes out in those dark red scarred letters: "The Horror of Chadbourne" with the music in the background that slams into your soul, so loud and sour, a dirge of finality, you wonder what to expect next.

We can thank Rick Hautala for this Chadbourne horror.

Yes, Rick Hautala. Rick is the wizard that waved his wand, aligned the planets and made sure that the Cthulhu gods took notice of Glenn Chadbourne's horrific and intricate art lo those many years ago. I have always associated these two fellows together in life since Rick brought Glenn into the fold. Two of the nicest guys you'd ever see together. Brothers from different mothers, but brothers all the same.

Who is Glenn Chadbourne? Glenn – he's like you and me – normal folk that took a different turn somewhere along the way. Oh, and he's got one helluva bent imagination. He makes our nightmares come to life on paper and then some.

You take one look at Glenn and you're not sure what to expect. He does give himself away though: it's his t-shirts. Horror on every-single-one-of-them. You can spot Glenn walking towards you blocks away with the creature features he adorns on the front of his self. I'd dare say if you catch him out at night, some of those black cotton tees glow as well.

Not that you'd find him out at night. He's too busy working.

Every time we speak he's working on this project for a long-time fan in Australia, or doing a quick cover for an independent press that has to have the art yesterday. Maybe even the day before that. Glenn takes it all on, and he delivers even if it means staying up late, and getting up early. I dare say that's not fireplace smoke coming out of the chimney at his house, it's from those little sticks he can't give up. "Dave," he says, "I've given up everything else in this world, but smokin' is the one thing I can say is mine and it's here to stay." If you see smoke surrounding Glenn's home, then there is definitely a fire of creative energy brewing within. Heck I even expect some of these drawn creatures to come crawling out the door when Glenn steps outside for a break, holding onto his legs, ready to spring and spread his brand of horror on the world.

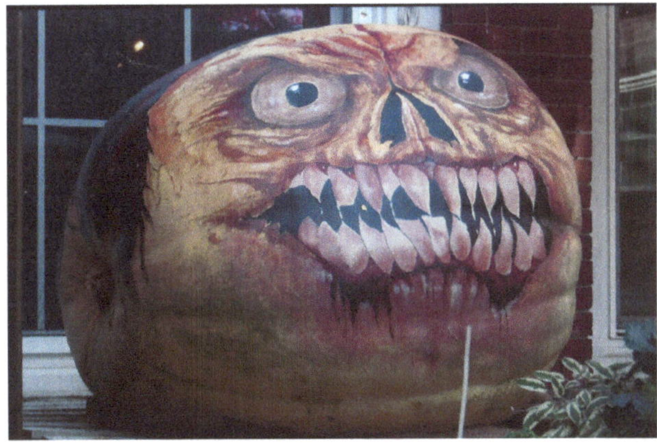

Glen Chadbourne's artwork will grab you. His detail from the in your face foreground images to the minute background detail, that is no less important, will suck you in. His pen and ink drawings I believe are more involved and engaging than some of his color work. However the pen and ink and the color form are two different sides of Glen Chadbourne and we're here to show a few of these sides here.

So I present to you a sampling of Glenn Chadbourne's work in the trade paperback you're holding in your eager hands. The full volume of "All's Not Well: The Gallery of Glenn Chadbourne" will be published in the Fall of 2013 in a much larger hard cover collection, all in color, and with many unique and unseen pieces as well as a history of this extraordinary artist's work. You'll be surprised at what's about to be unleashed.

Thank you Rick for bringing us a gifted artist, and an amazing friend to the horror community. Your efforts live on in so many of us. We miss you my man.

Thank you Glenn for all the twists and turns that you've presented to us here in this sampler, and to the many surprises you've brought us over the years. Let the horror continue my friend.

Have you ever thought about a creature oozing from the humid fog of a Lovecraft-New Orleans?

I'm sure you have.

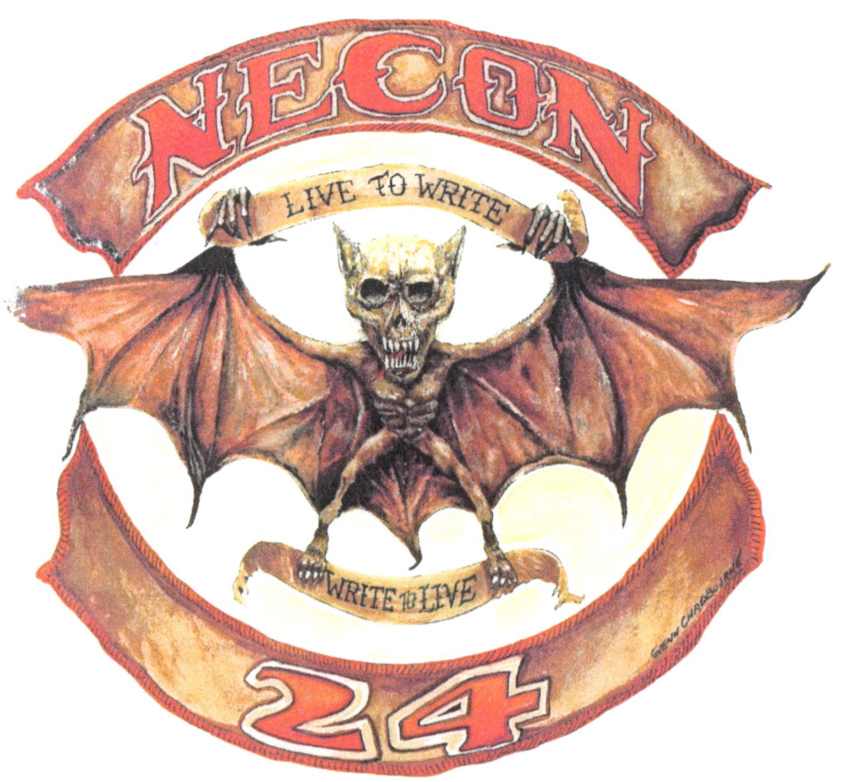

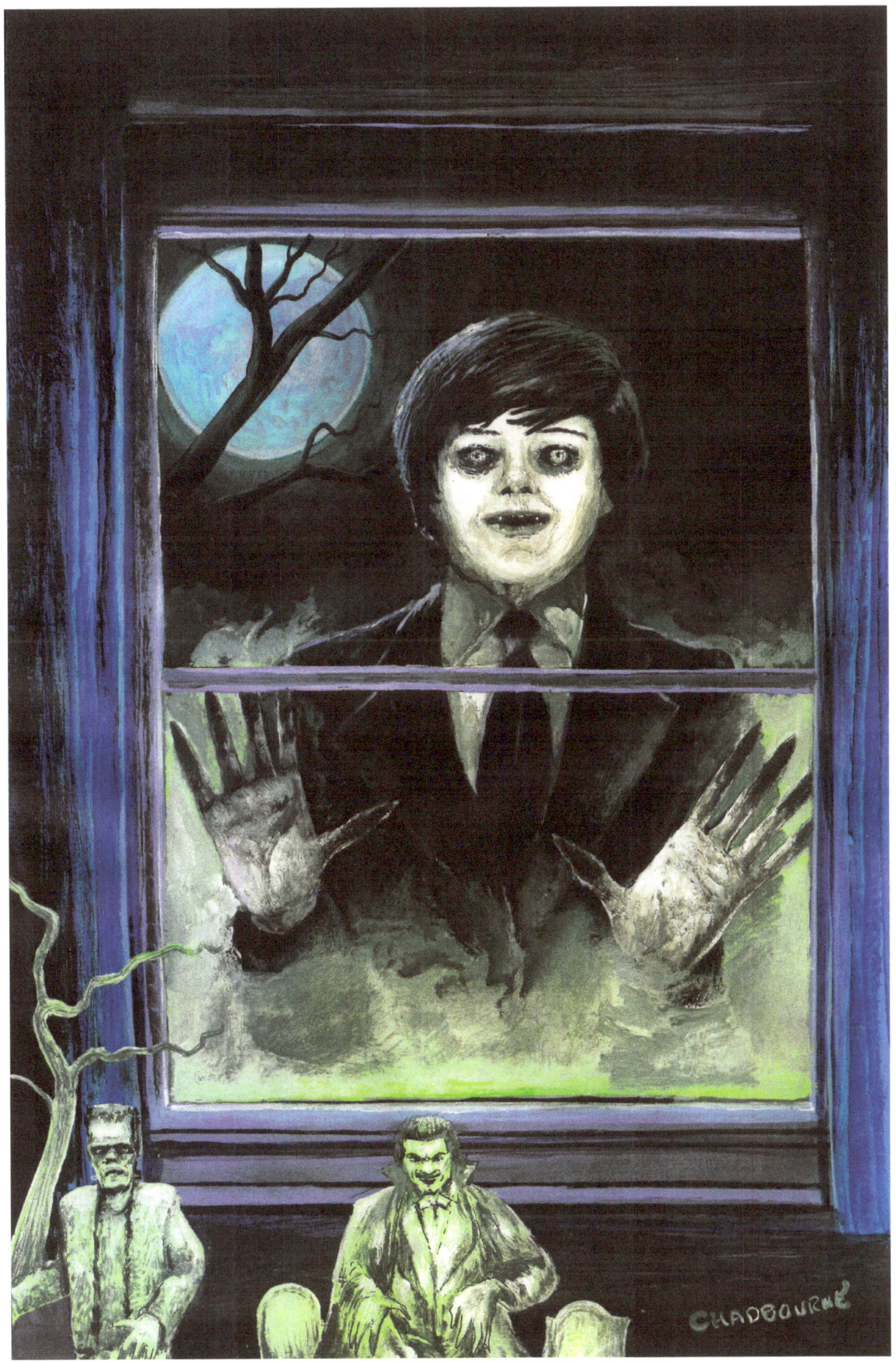
CHADBOURNE

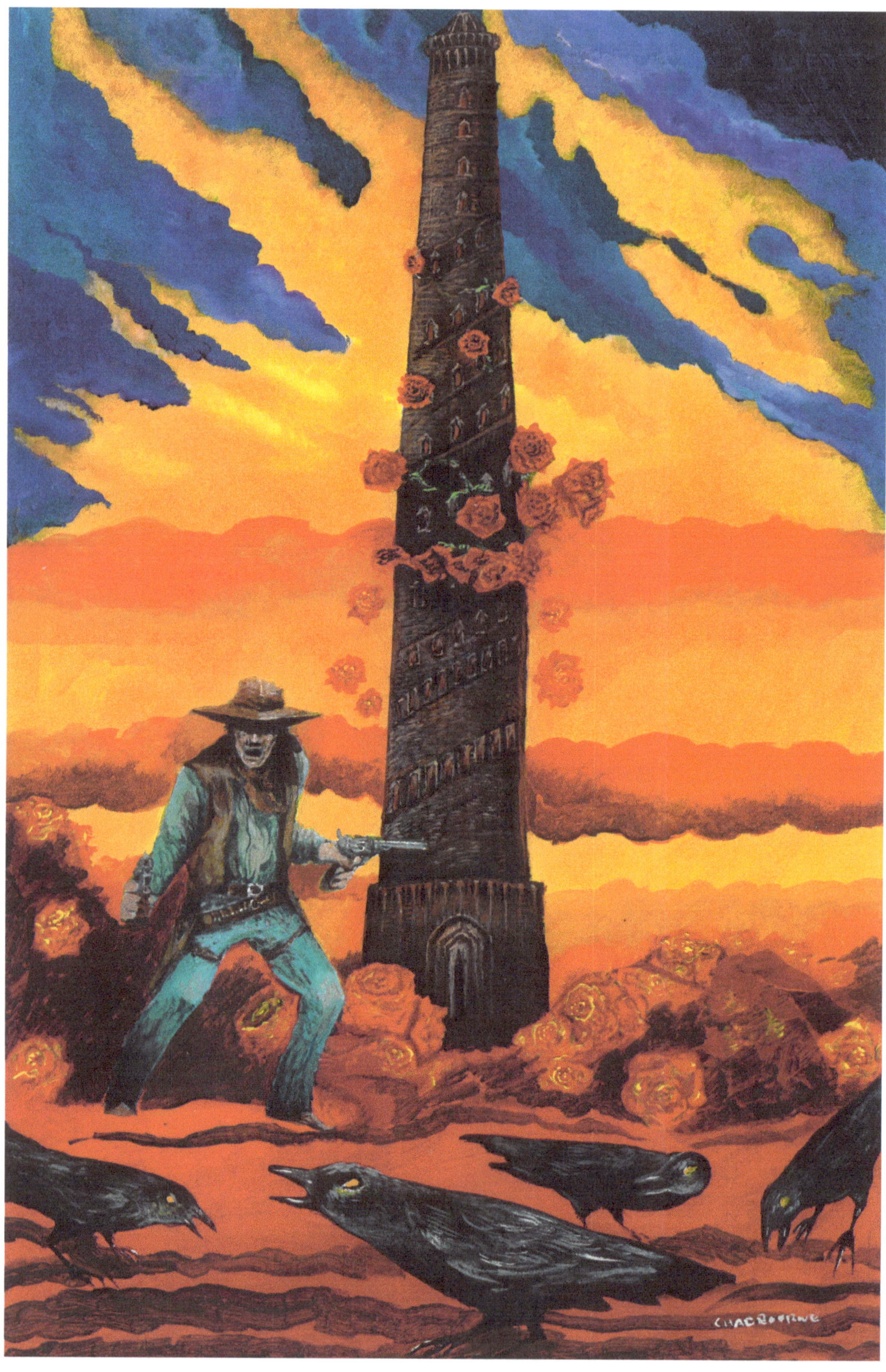

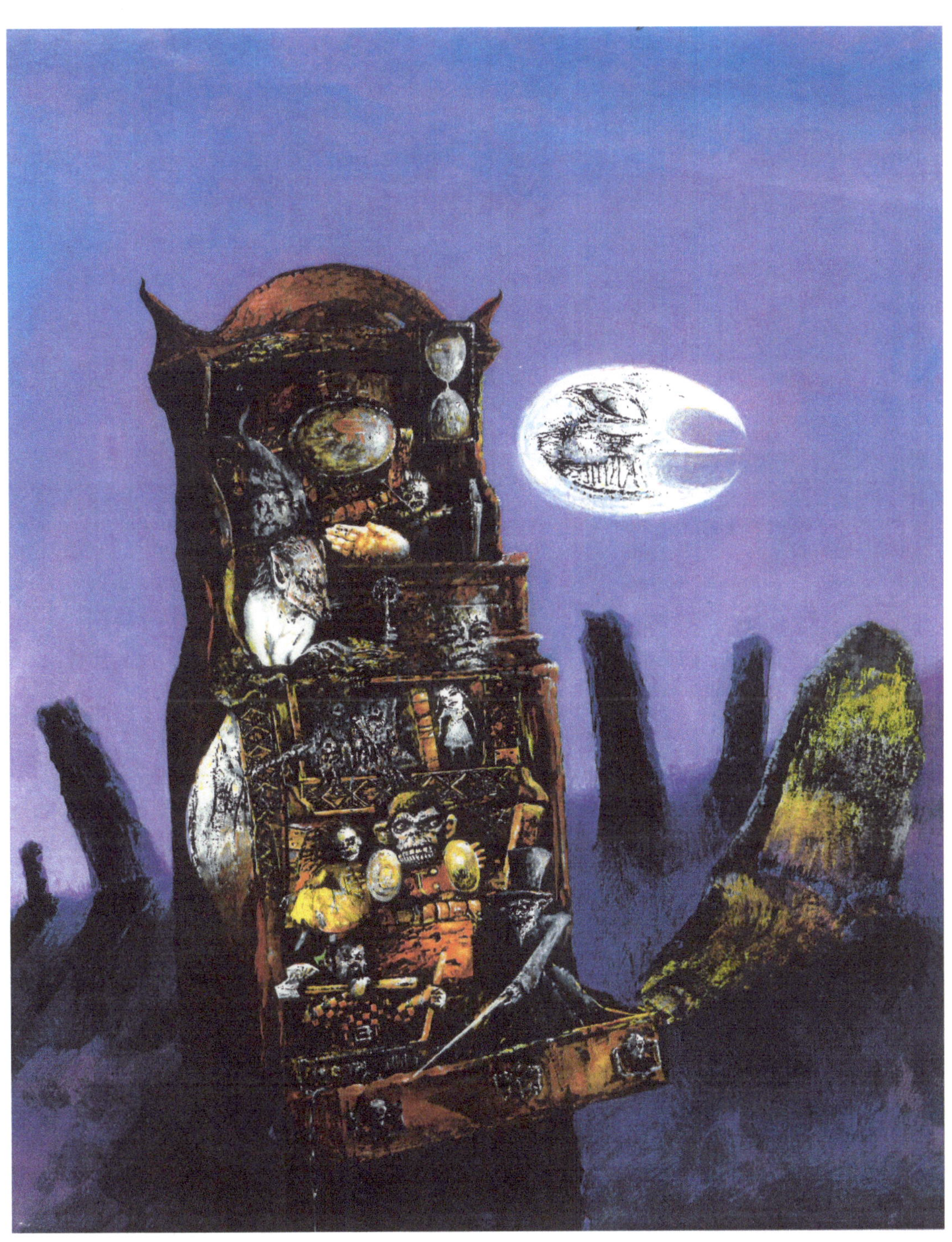

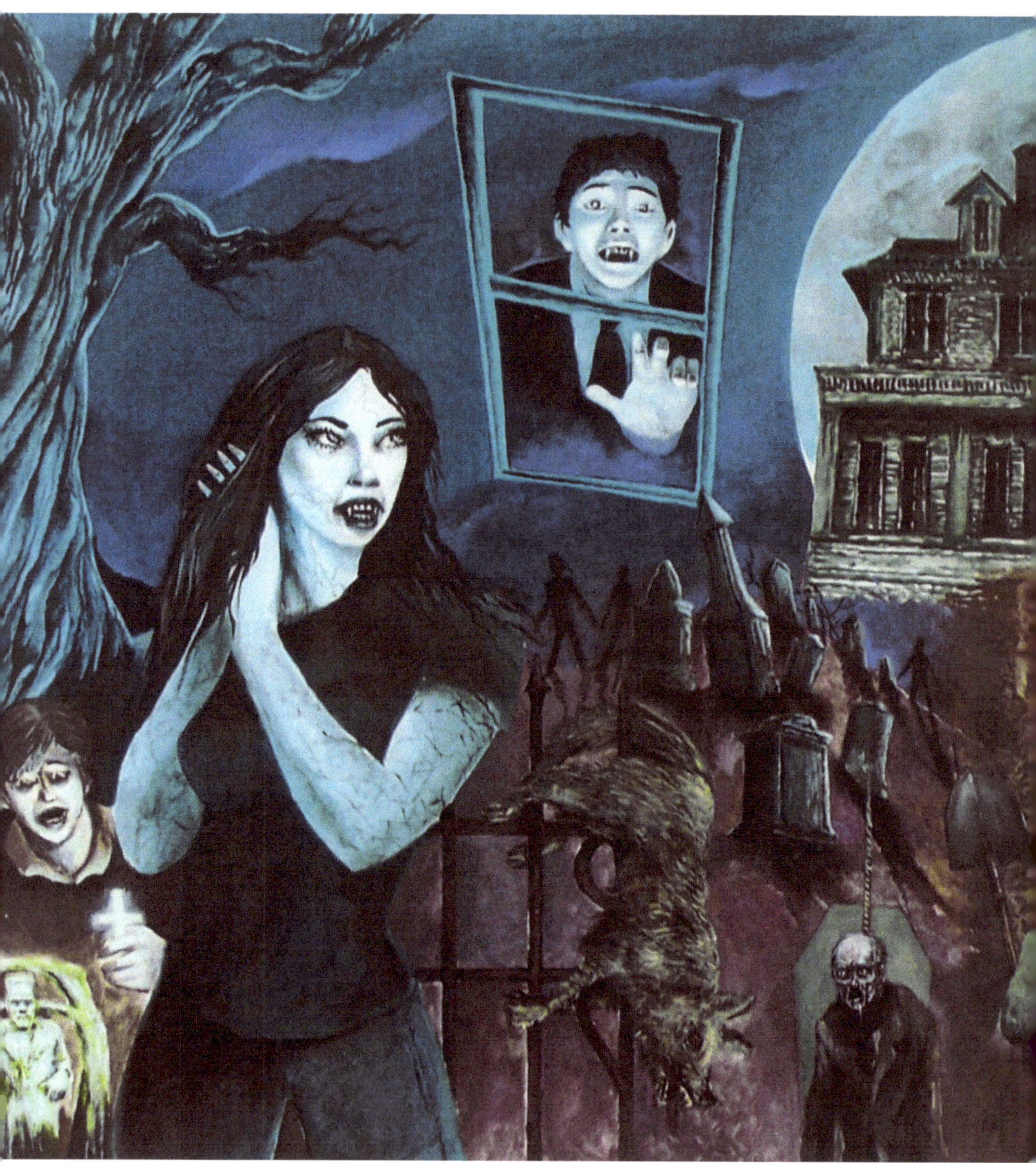

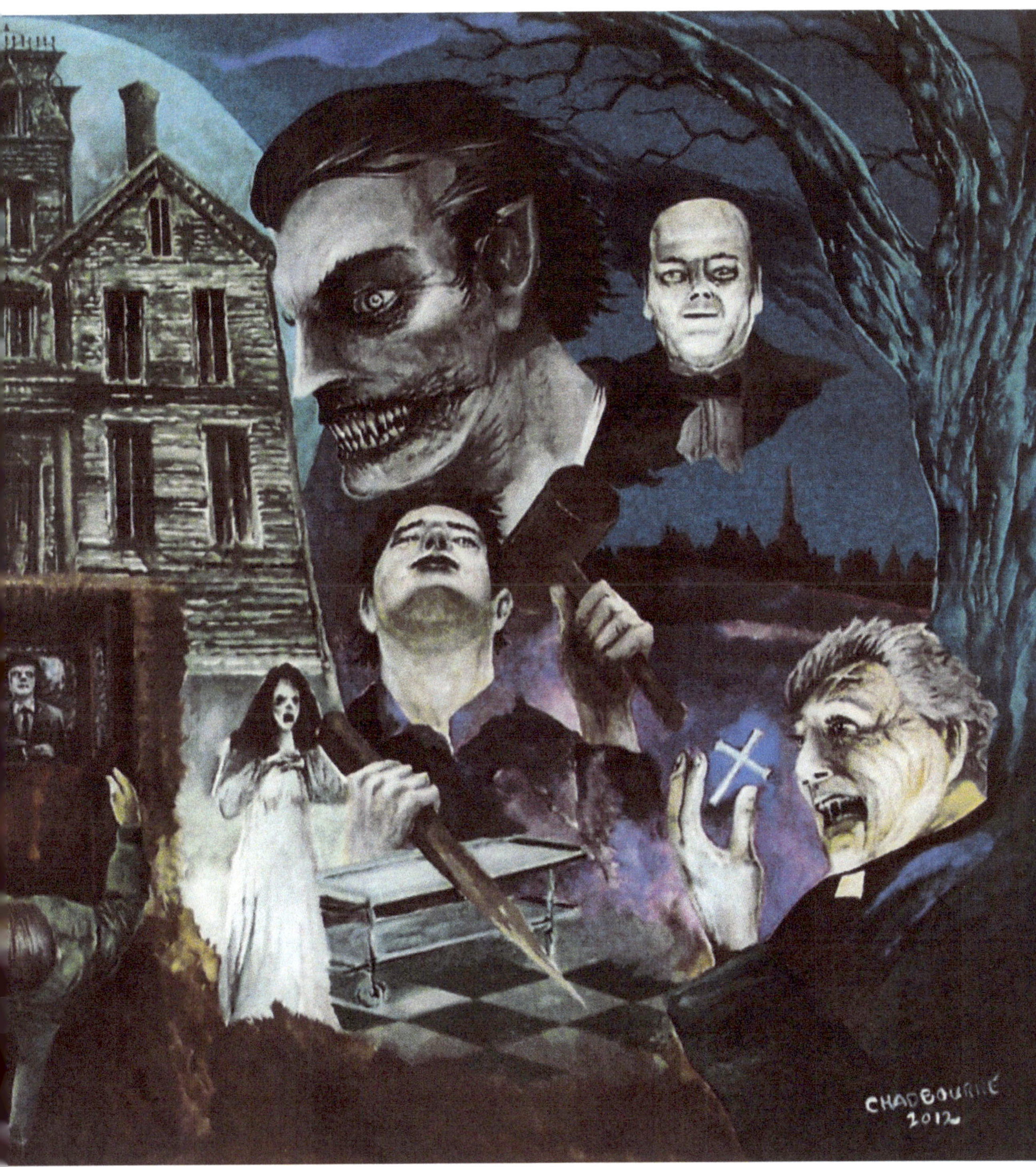
CHADBOURNÉ
2012

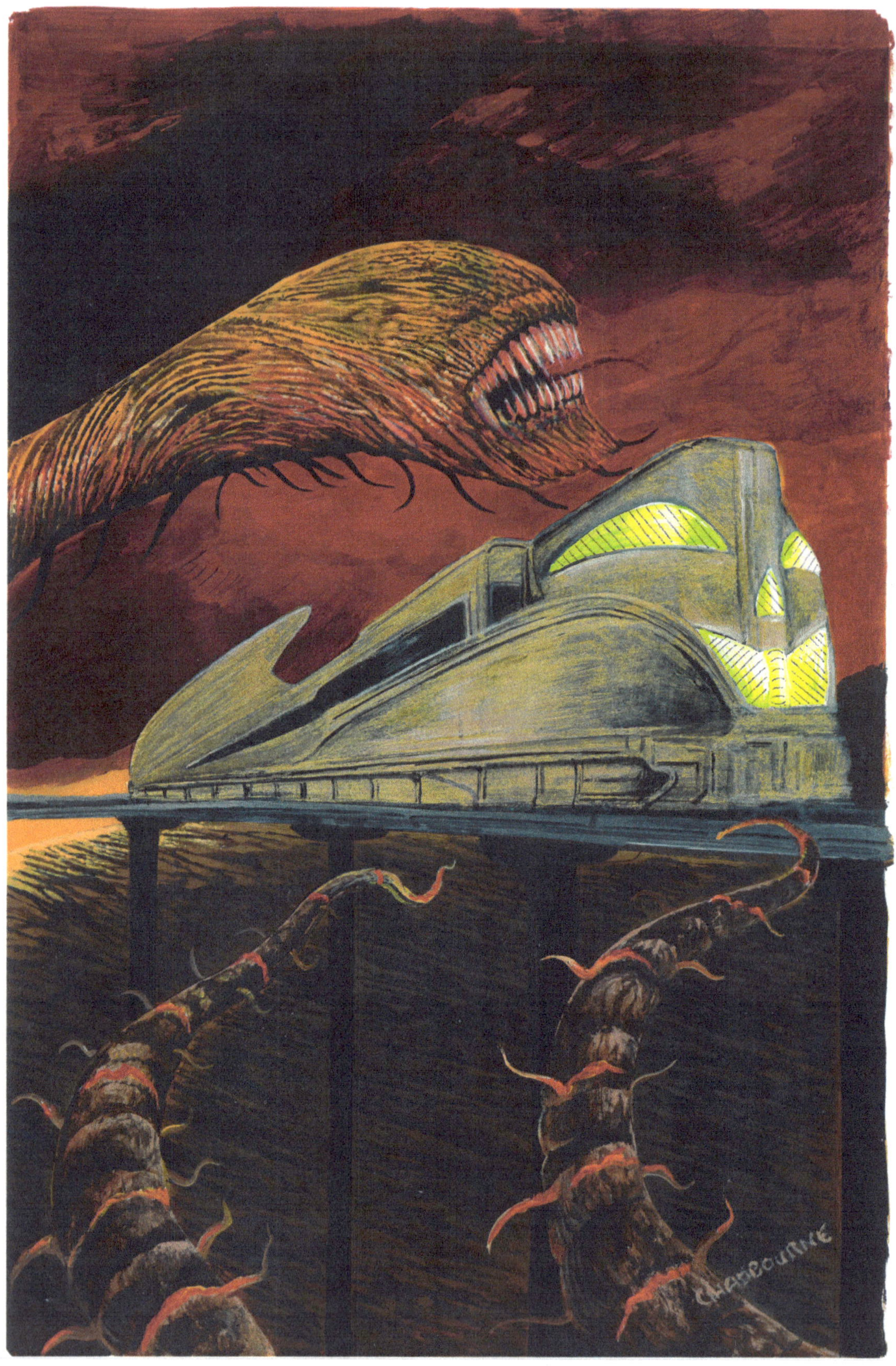
CHADBOURNE

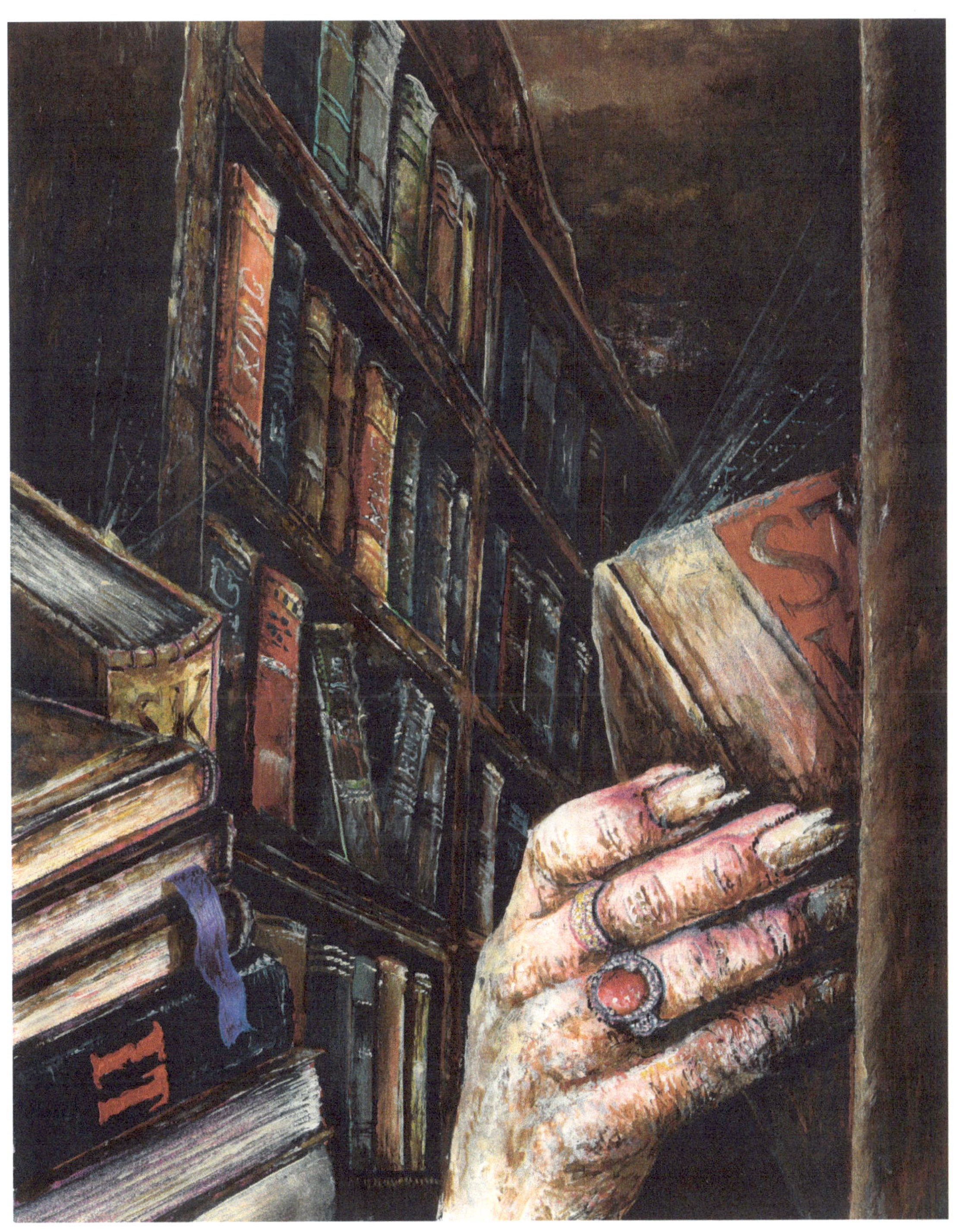
KING
IT

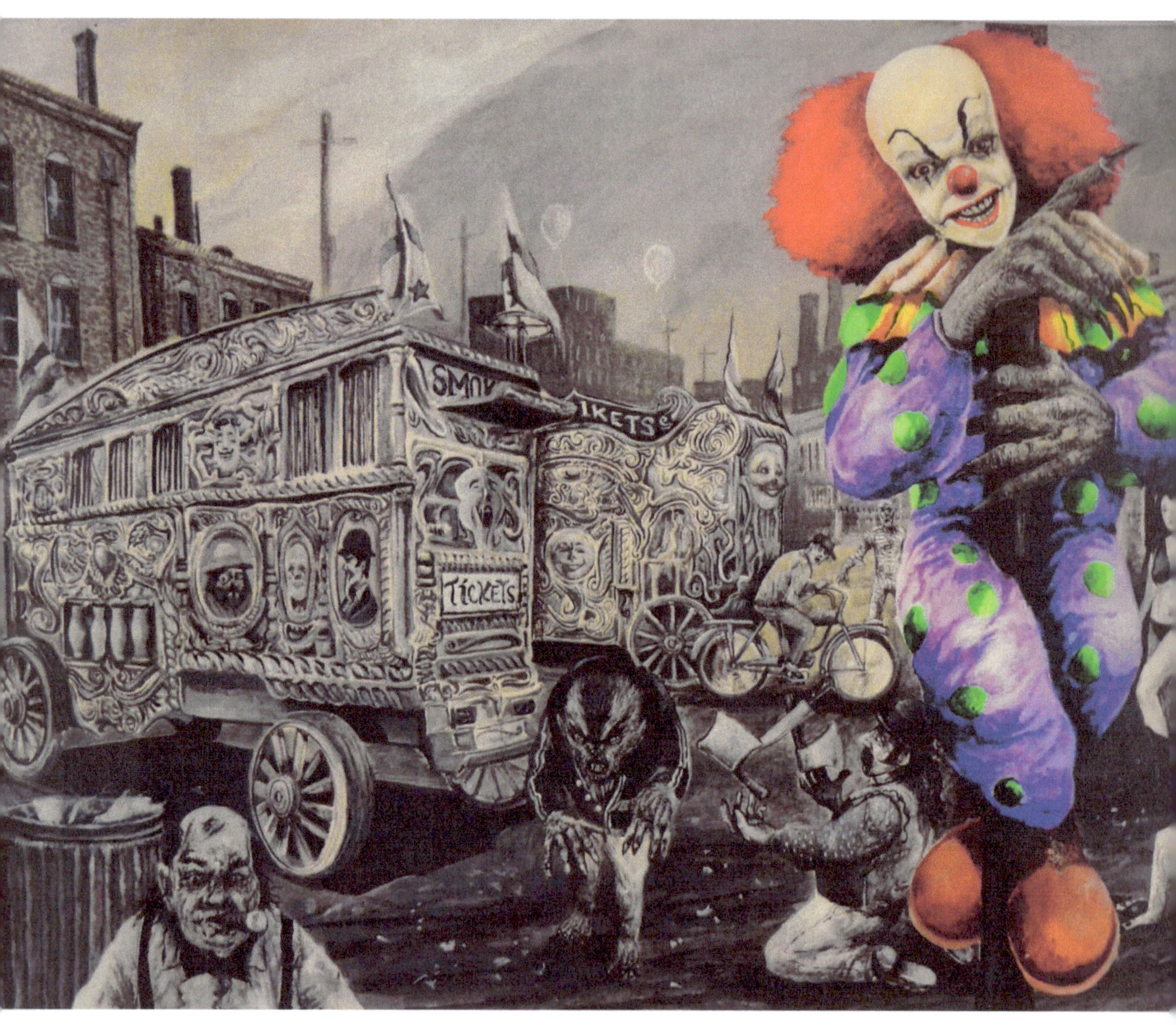
TICKETS

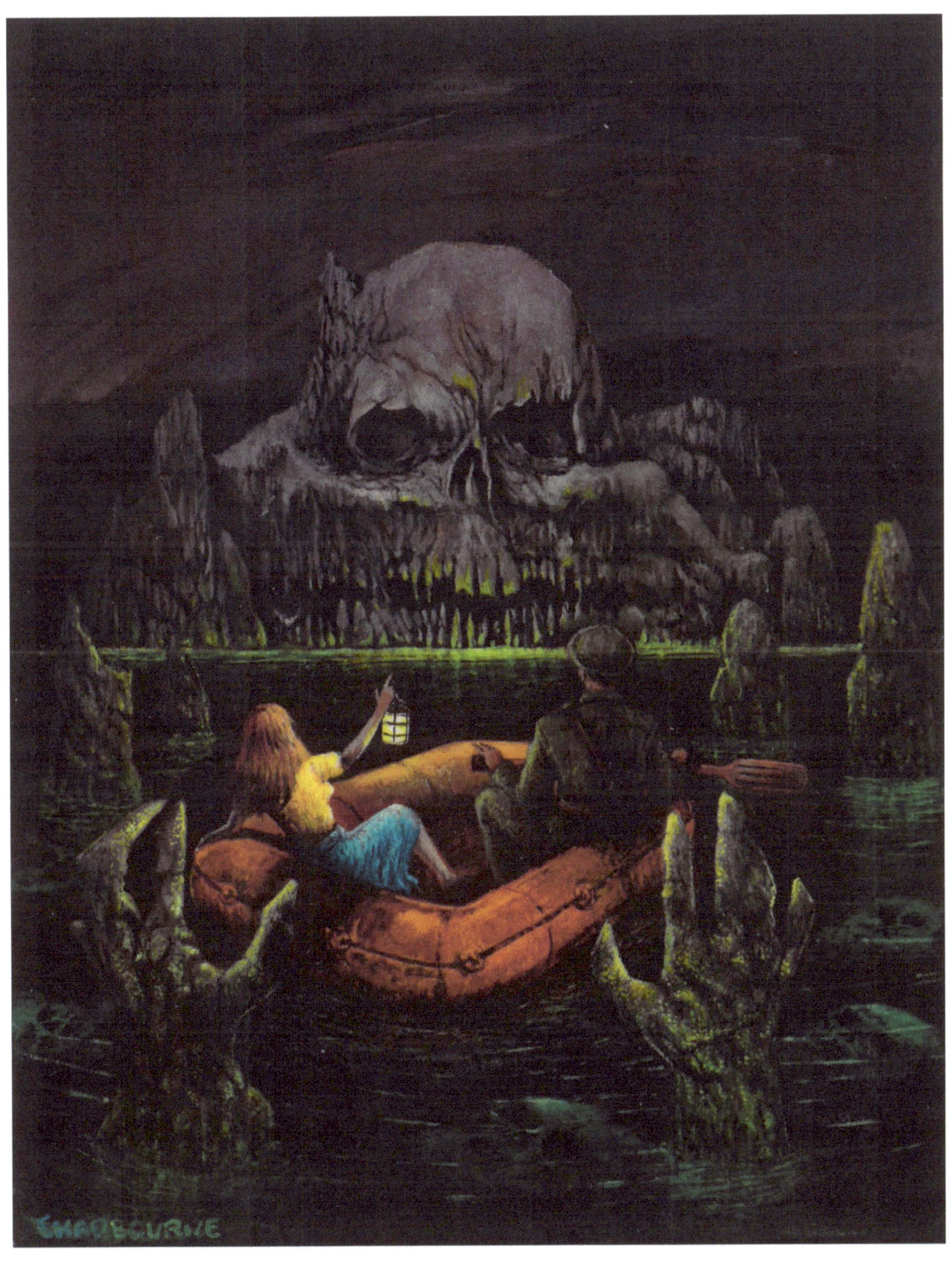
CHADBOURNE

DEEP SIX

By Glenn Chadbourne and Holly Newstein

Her face, pearl white and nearly translucent, shone like a tiny moon in the tangled mesh of the net. Her eyes mirrored her fear in dark, liquid pools. They darted from one man's face to the next as they loomed above her in the shadowed darkness. Great lumbering slabs of meat they were, gawking down at her, studying, measuring.

The moon dipped into view from the hole above her, and she could see their toothy, foul grins in the dim silver light. Their faces were cruel and mindless, like sharks, their clothing half-off even in the cold night air.

They had all taken a shot at her, every one of them, but it was hard because she was slippery, and the small slit of her sex was hidden beneath rows of slick scales. She had fought them hard, thrashing and bucking in the net, slashing with her incredibly strong tail, the fins sharp as razors. But still, they kept coming, again and again, slamming into her with their crushing weight, stinking of putrid bait and land things. And when they could not have her, their lust turned to rage.

They beat her with their gaffs, and she screamed. Her mouth, full and generous, splayed open wide then snapped closed, making a clacking sound when her teeth came together. The gillslits on either side of her slender throat expanded as she sought oxygen from the useless air.

She was dying, and as she died she began to sing.

Her song went straight into the men's heads, into their minds, as it had always been. Her song was a siren's song on a moonlit night, exquisite and intoxicating. They stopped beating her and listened to her sing, watched her final wracking efforts to free herself from the scraps of net that still pinned her. Her delicate, webbed fingers with their long nails shining like mother-of-pearl clawed vainly at the tangled mesh, her pointed teeth tore and gnashed at it. They stood stock-still, gaff hooks clutched in their hands, their hearts thundering, their own breaths boiling up out of the fish-hold in clouds that disappeared into the night sky.

In time, the song stopped. She lay still, shrouded in the coarse net. The men gently untangled her bruised, limp body and carried her from the hold onto the aft deck of the boat. Then they cast her back into the sea. They watched her sink, watched her alien, beautiful face vanish slowly into the inky blackness of the water.

As the corpse spiraled down into the depths, the memory of her song drifted through their minds, conjuring images of worlds filled with her kind, bright shimmering places alive with pale figures that moved with sinuous grace, beckoning to them and calling, always calling to them. They leaned over the side of the boat, staring into the dark waters long after she disappeared from view, trying to see down, down to her world. The bitter cold and dark of the landlocked world weighed heavily on them, and they were overcome with a terrible longing for the beauty and peace promised by her song.

And so, at length, they joined her.

All but one.

#

Harold Miller stared out at the deepening twilight that closed in around the *Sheila C.* His watch had stopped dead sometime before dawn, he supposed, but all he knew was that somehow he had lost almost eighteen hours.

He edged the boat's throttle slightly forward, coaxing up a few more horses from the engine, then took a slow turn to starboard. Thick gouts of salt spray frothed the windshield and sheets of sleet buffeted the wheelhouse.

He had come to, standing there at the wheel, his body numb with cold and his mind utterly empty. He had no memory of how he'd gotten there or what he was supposed to be doing.

A ghost of his own reflection stared back at him from the windshield as gray turned to deeper gray, and then black.

"Way down below the ocean…where I wanna be, she may be…"

The sound of his own voice surprised him, especially the sound of his own voice singing a stupid old song like "Atlantis." He always hated it when songs stuck in his head, but this one was persistent. The more he tried not to think of it, the louder it got.

"Wheeeere I wanna be…"

The swells were building, gaining height and volume, and edging at a faster clip. The Sheila C. began to roll at a sharper angle. The wind had picked up and changed direction while he'd been passed out or unconscious or whatever he had been. It was blowing nor'east now, bitch-cold and mean. He flipped on the running lights and could see ice caking the forward lines and the bow. Harold was sure the gear was already thick with it. It wasn't uncommon for ice to build up to two, even three feet along hulls and gear this time of year, caking every hatch and line, and turning whole vessels into solid blocks of cumbersome slag that were hell to maneuver. It was a steady battle to keep ahead of the ice, and often enough a boat would lose her electronics to a heavy buildup.

Harold figured he couldn't have passed out because there wasn't a drop of alcohol on the Sheila C. The captain on Harold's last boat – a guy from Cliff Island by the name of Ned Bedford Spruill – always brought a case or two of beer aboard for the crew to share on their way home to port. The Cap' was clever about it—he'd stow the beer in the hold, then take on the ice for the trip. The beer would be buried under a ton of ice. When all the ice had been shoveled into the hold to chill the fish they'd caught, they knew it was time to head home, and cans would be passed all around.

It was something to look forward to.

Harold wished he hadn't quit the last boat, but there wasn't enough money there. Of course, there was no beer here. But money or not, if he'd stayed with Captain Spruill, he wouldn't have lost eighteen hours of his life and be stuck out in the North Atlantic with a nor'easter coming and no clue what the hell was going on.

He kept staring out into the darkness, feeling the boat lug against the strain of the swells and the ice. A voice squawked from the radio and made Harold jump:

"Camden Marine calling the *Sheila C.* Come in, *Sheila C.*"

It was Dale Prescott, the boat's owner.

"*Sheila C.* Come in, *Sheila C.*"

Harold stared stupidly at the radio.

"Way downnnn below the ocean..."

"Lamar? You there? Pick up.

"Where I wanna be..."

"Lamar? Richards? Anybody there? Miller?"

"...she may be..."

"When are you idiots coming back in? Wilfred? Anyone there? Pick up for Chrissakes!"

Harold gathered himself with an effort. He had to pick up, to say something, or Prescott would call the Coast Guard. He picked up and thumbed the mic open.

"Just heading in now ... We're full up."

Sleet continued to buffet against the windows, but it was invisible now, just a steady rhythmic pattern in tune with the churn of the engines. His ghost stared back at him from the windshield, limned in green from the glow of the instrument lights.

Just heading in now...we're full up, mimed the ghost.

Last Harold could recall, there wasn't a single herring in the hold.

He stared into the blank face and empty eyes of his *doppelganger,* which stared right back. He would not have been at all surprised if his ghost-reflection suddenly broke eye contact, grabbed the open mic, and began screaming to Prescott, screaming into the blackness that something was wrong, terribly wrong.

Harold switched off the radio. He raised his hand and traced the face in the windshield.

Something is wrong, he thought. *You're fuckin-A right about that, my friend.*

I wish to fuck I knew what.

Something banged from below, and Harold whirled around. Something loud. Something big. The sound echoed up through the open hatch leading to the bunk area—"the doghouse," the crew called it—and the small galley.

Thok...thok...thok!

His eyes fixed on the dark square that led below. Ice had begun to form on the metal ladder that led down. It gleamed in the glow of the running lights. He realized the temperature had dropped sharply in the wheelhouse, and he hadn't even noticed it. He continued to stare into the open hatchway as he fished in his coat pocket for his cigarettes, but the pack was soaked to mush. The cigarettes were ruined.

When did this happen? he thought.

The radio squawked. Harold turned back to the wheel. The radio power switch was turned to OFF, but the power light still glowed green.

I turned that damned thing off, I know I did. The switch must be fucked.

He focused on listening for the sound below to repeat. A low voice hissed from the radio, barely audible over the wind. The signal was full of static and broken, as if it came from far away.

"Miller? You there, Miller?"

But it wasn't Prescott's voice.

Harold stared at the radio and puffed out a cloud of breath.

Someone's screwing around, he thought. *Someone on shore, or some other fisherman. That bunch on the Jubilee, maybe. They heard Prescott calling, and now they want to play games, to spook me.*

He pulled the radio's plug from the receptacle, and the green power light winked out.

"Fuck you," Harold said. His voice sounded strained as it echoed in the wheelhouse. Almost crazed. Not like his own voice at all. He glanced up at the windshield, and for an instant he saw someone—or something—else in the ghost-reflection. A pale, delicate face, dark hair floating around it like seaweed, the eyes sunken and dull. A dead face. Then the image morphed back into his own familiar Viking's face, the long blonde hair tangled, soaked in salty clumps and clinging to the oil gear he wore.

How did I get so damned wet?

The thumping sound came again from below. Harold walked to the open hatch. He could barely hear anything over the wind and the creaking of the ice-laden rigging and the throbbing of the engines. But that was the thing. Whatever was banging around down there was loud enough to sound over everything.

He listened intently.

It came again, echoing through the small passage that ran below.

Thok! Thok! THOK!

Louder this time. Like something grating rhythmically against the hull. But not grating...beating. And not from the inside. From the outside.

Impossible.

But was it?

The gear...the lines must still be out.

It was possible that the gear had gotten fouled alongside or under the boat. While he was unconscious, the boat easily could have crossed over the lines, could have dragged enormous lengths of coiled chain and matted netting into a nest of tangled weight under the hull. If the lines fed into the prop, he'd be screwed; if they were snarled under the hull, he'd have to free them. Maybe even cut them away. But in this weather, a job like that would be difficult and dangerous. And there was nobody else on board to help him.

Nobody else.

The realization that he was alone on the boat finally filtered into his fogged-in brain. It hit him like a belly blow, and he staggered against the wheel.

While he'd been unconscious, the others had abandoned the *Sheila C.* and left him to his fate.

Vanished.

Why?

Dimly, a memory began to form and then break up, like confetti in the wind. He knew where they had gone—into the ocean.

But why, damnit?

He began singing, hoarsely.

"Way downnn below the ocean...where I wanna be...she may be..."

The wind snatched at his words, pulling them from his cracked lips.

THOK! THOK! THOK!

He could see a cloud of steam rising in the wheelhouse from the open hatch. Except it wasn't steam—steam was hot, and this stuff was cold and clammy, colder even than the air in the wheelhouse. It was thick, milky-white and salty, and it smelled sickly. Like rancid, rotting fish. A shudder arced up his spine into his neck.

The power light on the radio glowed green again, and a voice came from the speaker. Harold recognized the voice this time. It was Bobby Lamar, skipper of the *Sheila C.*

"Miller? You there, Millerrrrrrrr?" Lamar's voice had an icy, faraway tone. "The nets, Miller...remember the nets...you have to free the nets."

Harold reeled back from the radio as if he'd been bitten and crashed up against the wheel. The sharp plywood corner of the control panel pierced through his oil gear and gouged his lower back, but he hardly felt it. He saw the dead face in the windshield again. This time it turned its glazed eyes and stared at him with a look of dumb sorrow.

Bobby Lamar's voice reverberated in the wheelhouse. "Reeeemember, Miller, the nets … have to haul the nets … reeeemember!

Wham! Wham! WHAM!

The pounding was deafening. Harold slipped on a patch of ice and sprawled on the deck. The pounding on the hull echoed in his brain. He bit at his hand without realizing, drawing blood, and stifling back a scream.

"Reeeememberrrrr…" squawked the radio.

And all at once Harold did remember.

#

"I said move it! Move your ass! You want your fucking paycheck, right?"

Bobby Lamar's long ponytail played out from the hooded sweatshirt he wore under his foul-weather gear. It streamed out and flapped wildly in the wind, coal-black threaded with silver-gray. His cheeks and brow were chapped and blotchy, and his eyes glittered in their darkened hollows.

"You hear me, Miller?"

Harold said nothing, just kept his eyes on the lines as they played out with a steady whine through the big spool.

"You ain't much, Miller. You know that? Not much a'tall!"

Bobby Lamar and the other five crewmembers had been on his ass ever since he began working aboard the *Sheila C.* three weeks ago. He knew it went that way with boats and crews sometimes. Fishermen were a superstitious group, and Harold was the new man here. So he was the butt of every joke, and the target of everyone's frustration.

But this bunch was the worst Harold had ever seen. The only thing keeping him from quitting was that the *Sheila C.* was a money boat. It was an earner, always had been, and Harold could overlook a lot when it came to money. However, the last few trips had been off weight—poor, to say the least—and of course it was Harold's fault.

Wilfred Townshend screamed at Harold from the aft shucking house.

"Miller! Get a hose on that gurry slatherin' up the hold! Fuckin' thing smells like your old lady's cunt! And I'd know!"

The *Sheila C.* had been previously set up as a scallop dragger, and the small shucking house had stayed when they'd rigged the boat over for groundfishing. It was a good wind block.

"Smells like fish, eat it!" hollered Tommy Hanscomb from somewhere forward.

Harold wished, more than ever now, that he'd never left Captain Spruill's boat and his beer. He vowed he'd settle the score with this ugly bunch of loudmouthed assholes. But not today...not here.

"Never mind the hold!" snapped Bobby Lamar over the drone of the engine's exhaust. "You just watch the feed on that fuckin' spool! Get those lines set and don't screw around ... there's heavy weather comin' in."

The spool reeled out the last lengths of net, and when it was clear, Harold winched it to a stop. They were set to tow. He signaled Buddy Pelsot in the wheelhouse, and the *Sheila C.* began a slow turn to starboard. This would be the third tow of the day. There was nothing to show for the first two, and Harold grimaced, thinking how bad things would be if the nets came up empty yet again. He fervently hoped the herring would be where they were supposed to be, and things would settle down to dull monotony for a while.

Harold double-checked the set, then stepped back and looked around. Wilfred and Tommy were smoking a joint in the shucking house. Bobby Lamar had gone up to the wheelhouse with Buddy, and the Tilton brothers, who had fished the boat the longest with Lamar, were up forward somewhere.

Least they've found something else to do other than bust my balls, Harold thought.

There was indeed some weather coming in from the northeast. The sea had turned a steely gray, and foamy whitecaps frosted the swells. While working the spool, Harold had managed to soak two sweatshirts and a pair of canvas overalls through, even under his oil gear. He knew if he didn't go below and change into dry clothes, the clothes he wore now would freeze solid. There was at least half an hour before they began pulling the nets back, so he made his way forward, past the shucking house to the wheelhouse hatch that led below deck. Twenty minutes later he was back at the spool, smoking a cigarette.

The lines continued to play in. They were nearly at the end. Bobby signaled to Tommy Hanscomb to take his spot at the boom. It was time to haul in what they'd caught. Harold gave Captain Lamar a thumbs-up and motioned to Tommy that the lines were at their end. Tommy engaged the boom lever, and the big net broke the surface. It fed slowly up past the spool and beyond. Seawater poured from the net in rivers, and for the first time since they'd left dock in Webwick nearly three days earlier, there was a frenzy of movement in the net. It was alive with herring, tens of thousands of shiny bodies twisting and flipping in the prison mesh.

The net continued along, high over the deck toward the open hold; then Tommy Hanscomb threw the boom lever forward, and the net lowered down.

Herring rained into the hold—and so did something else.

Something larger.

Something extraordinary.

They all saw it.

"What the—" Tommy muttered. He had seen the swipe of a good-sized tail covered with iridescent green and blue scales. He stood at the edge of the hold, staring down into the darkness. Lamar made his way along the deck and joined Tommy. He, too, stared down into the hold, his head cocked like a dog's.

"Whaddya think, Cap? Big shark or tuna?" Tommy's voice was distant. "Maybe one of them manatees?"

"Ain't no manatee," Lamar replied absently. "Ain't no ..."

As Harold watched, the two men began swaying in unison at the edge of the hold, moving to a beat he could not hear. He stepped forward, afraid they were going to fall in. He saw Bobby Lamar's jaw begin to spasm.

"Fetch me a gaff," he suddenly roared.

The Tiltons hurried forward, both carrying gaff hooks. Lamar took one mechanically. "Shut down the gear," he shouted. "Shut everything down!"

The other men had all gathered around the hold, forming a loose circle. Harold stood on the outside, peering over their shoulders. It was early evening now, and the full moon broke from behind the clouds. He could see the deep pile of herring boiling in the hold, obscuring whatever the larger creature was that had come in the net with them.

"What the fuck?" repeated Tommy, in that same dreamy voice.

"What the fuck is going on here?" echoed Harold.

Lamar climbed cautiously down the rungs of the ladder, slowly, into the darkness of the hold. The herring swarmed around him up to his knees, and he kicked at the fish to clear a path that filled in as quickly as it opened before him. The larger creature bucked in the center of the hold, sending geysers of fish in every direction. It was coiled up in a fold of net. Lamar reached forward warily and gripped the net entangling it. Harold held his breath, knowing that whatever it was likely had a set of nasty teeth and would be pissed off enough to use them.

Lamar cut away the net with his shucking knife. A strange scent filled the hold and wafted out to the men above. It was sweet and intoxicating and like nothing Harold had ever smelled before. His vision clouded, and all he could see were star-shaped flashes of white light. His head swam as if he'd just finished off a bottle of Jack Daniels. His blood pulsed in his temples and rushed to his groin.

Shit! Why the fuck am I getting turned on? Hot for herring, f'crissakes!

With a huge effort, he stepped back and away from the hold, and his head cleared. He knuckled his eyes until they came back into focus, and he looked around at his shipmates.

The Tiltons were naked from the waist down, holding their cocks in their hands. Their oil-gear was piled around their ankles, flapping like canvas sails on the deck as the icy wind blew around them. Tommy was completely naked. He ran his right hand along his chest, tweaking his own nipples as he stroked himself with his left. Wilfred was wearing nothing but his blue watch cap. He was moaning loudly, and his eyes had ridden so high in his head only the whites showed.

"Nearly got her!" Lamar howled from the hold. His voice was high-pitched and frenzied.

The Tiltons cackled wildly. Harold was speechless. He had no idea what was happening, but he knew it was bad.

They've all gone crazy!

He grabbed Wilfred's bare shoulder and spun him around. Wilfred looked astonished as he faced Harold. His chest was white and bony, covered with gooseflesh and acne that nearly fluoresced in the moonlight. He continued to work at himself even as he stared vacantly into Harold's face.

"What the *fuck* is wrong with you?" Harold barked. "What is it with all of you?"

"Leave go of me, Miller, you cocksucker! Leave go of me, or I'll kill yah! I swear I'll kill yah!" Wilfred pulled away from Harold's hand.

Tommy snapped his head around and met Harold's eyes. He had a vicious, stupid expression on his face. He leered at him, pinching his left nipple wickedly, and Harold remembered a mean whore he'd once known who stabbed a friend of his in the groin.

"Stay out of this," Tommy hissed. "Stay out of this. This is ours—all ours. You don't belong to this. You're not crew. You've brung the luck of Jonah on us!"

Harold glared back at Tommy.

"Blow me, you pissant fuckstick," he replied. Clearly they had all gone off the deep end, for whatever reasons. Harold decided to put in a call to the Coast Guard. He started to move over to the wheelhouse when Lamar shrieked. Harold turned back and stared, his eyes widening. The others crowded the opening, pounding at themselves; their heads arched back so the cords in their necks stood out like ropes. Hysterical shrieks and groans rose from the hold, and something else.

A glow.

A pale white glow.

The men all lurched as if they were climaxing as one and began leaping into the opening. Harold ran to the edge and looked down into the hold.

Lamar was straddling a mermaid. The others crowded around, their faces slack and vacant.

"Look at her," Lamar cooed. "Just look at her, would'ja? She's set my head on fire." He straddled her and gouged at her midriff with his thick right hand, kneading her belly and searching for her sex. His expression turned nasty, and he hissed down at the mermaid. "But where is it, you whore? Where's your cunny? Where's your thing?"

Harold could see the moon reflected in her dark, terrified eyes. He began to tremble.

Wilfred lumbered across the hold in three quick strides and booted Bobby in the head. The sound reverberated in the closed space. He pushed Bobby off the writhing girl just as Tommy grabbed his neck.

"Leave go of her! She's mine! *Mine*, damn yah!"

Tommy went wild on Wilfred, pounding on his back and ripping tufts of thinning hair from his head. The Tiltons joined in, and suddenly there was a frenzied brawl in the hold. The men wrestled each other, fighting to tear at the girl as she thrashed amid the bits of cut netting and dead herring. A man would gain a grip, only to lose it. At last, Lamar began to throw wild barnyard swings, batting the man from the girl. He pounded on her and got his fingers inside her by sheer chance.

"Gotcha! I gotcha!" Inside his head, Harold could hear the mermaid shrieking in agony and terror, an otherworldly, heartbreaking sound. He screamed in answer to her as the others fell on her, lapping, squeezing, tearing, sucking madly at every inch of her. She squirmed and bucked wildly.

And then she began to sing.

Harold spun away from the hold. He slipped on the wet deck and fell heavily, face first, soaking himself in the water that had poured off the net … off of her. He struggled to his feet and ran to the wheelhouse.

He grabbed the radio mic to call the Coast Guard … and stopped. A lovely sound was running through his head, blotting out everything else. He knew he'd wanted to do something important, but it just didn't seem so damned important anymore. Not as important as the lilting, hypnotic song.

He looked out at the starry night sky through the windshield. Then he closed his eyes.

#

"The lines, Miller … It's time to haul in the lines. See what you've caught."

Harold looked at his ghost-reflection and saw recollection on his face, followed by pain and terror.

"The lines, Miller … Remember the lines …" the radio squawked.

Slowly, Harold left the wheelhouse, working his way carefully over the ice-covered boat. When he got to the spool, he saw that, too, had a thick coating of ice. Still, when he kicked on the hydraulics, they worked just fine. The lines fed in slowly, and as they did, the song echoed faintly in his head again.

Such a beautiful song. Peaceful.

He listened with his eyes closed until he heard the net break the surface.

The bloated faces of the Tilton brothers came into view first as the net twirled overhead. Then Tommy Hanscomb's face, frozen in a leer. Wilfred Townshend's nose had been eaten away neatly while he'd been under, and Bobby Lamar was lacking his eyes. Eyes went quick in the sea, Harold knew. Things down there liked eyes.

How had the net come to play itself out with nobody aboard to operate the gear?

Perhaps *something* had slipped aboard to work it.

Perhaps *something* had gathered the men from below and brought them back—because they didn't belong down there.

It wasn't their world.

Dawn was coming now. The sky was streaked bloody red at the horizon where the storm clouds were breaking up. The sea was calmer; the wind abated. The net swung slowly overhead, dripping. One of Lamar's hands poked through the mesh with the index finger pointing stiffly at Harold as if accusing him of something.

Harold walked over to the boom lever and worked the gear. The net hovered along the deck until it passed over the hold. Then he dropped in the catch.

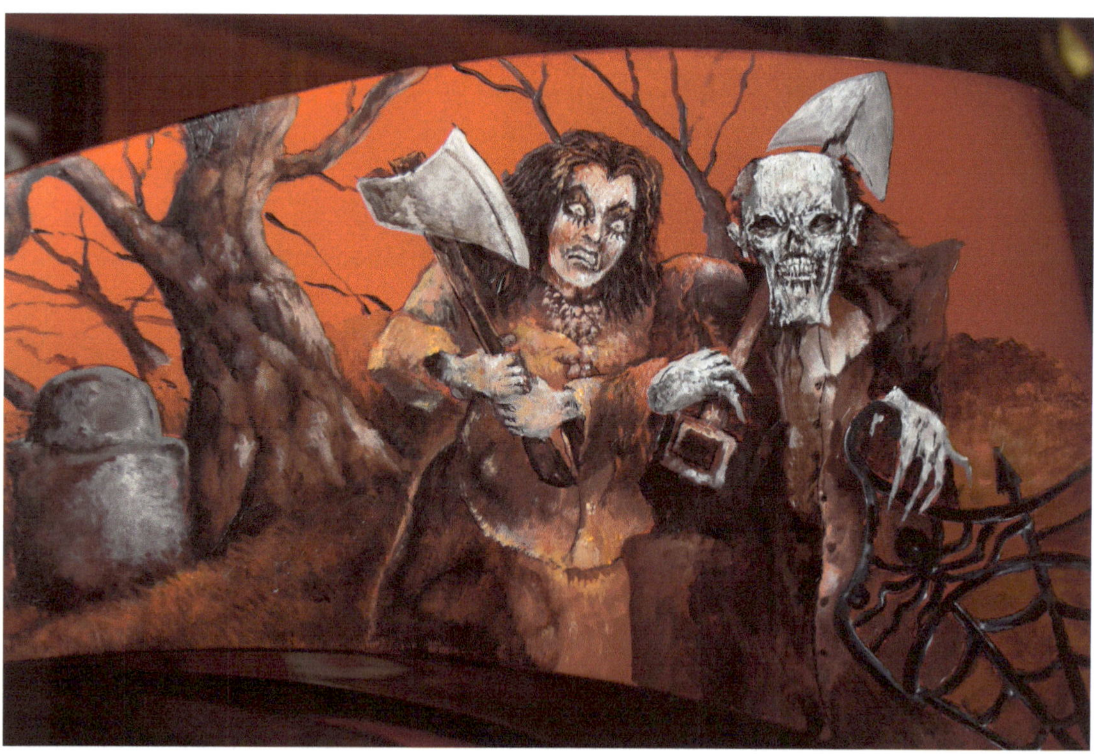

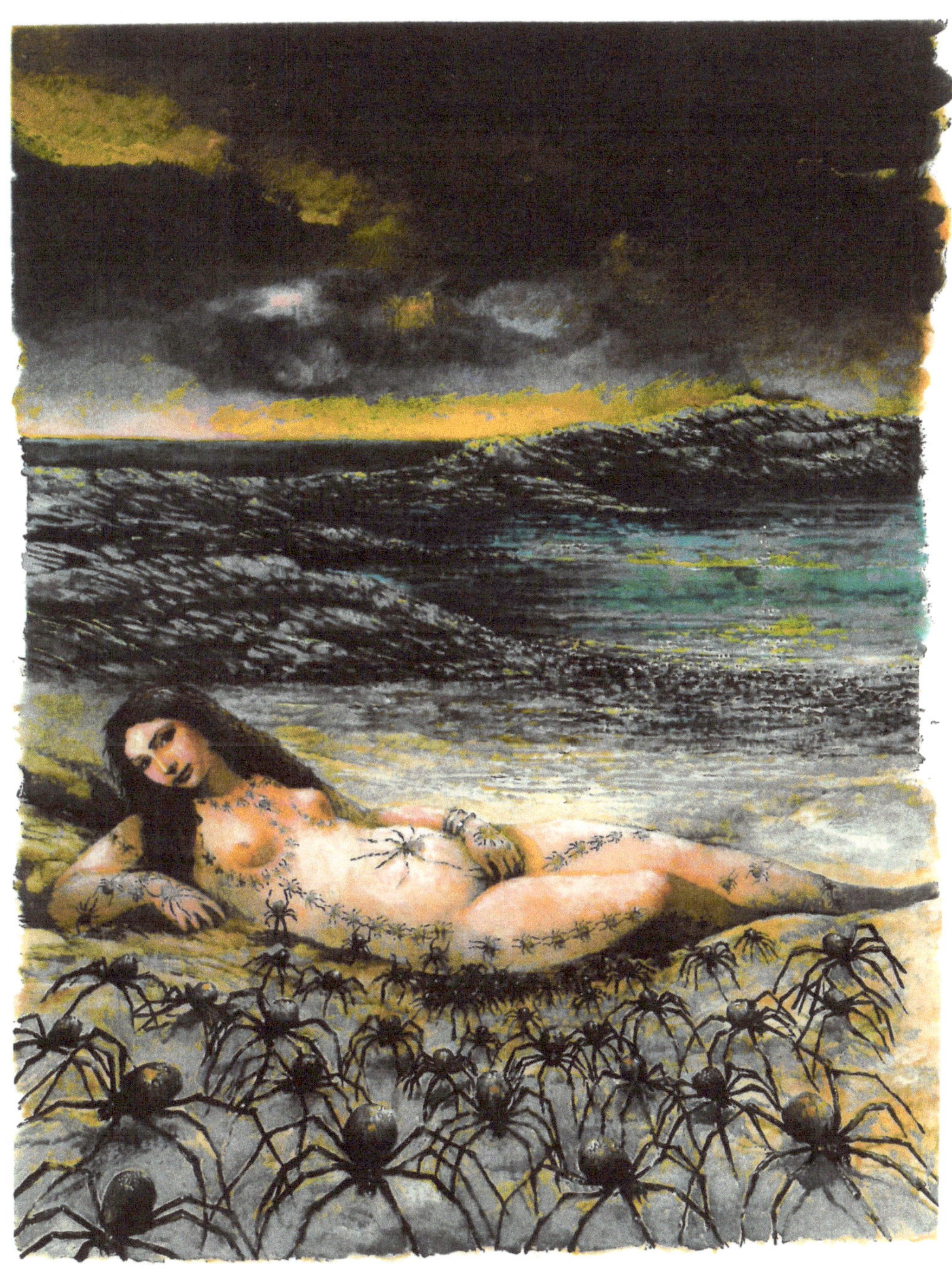

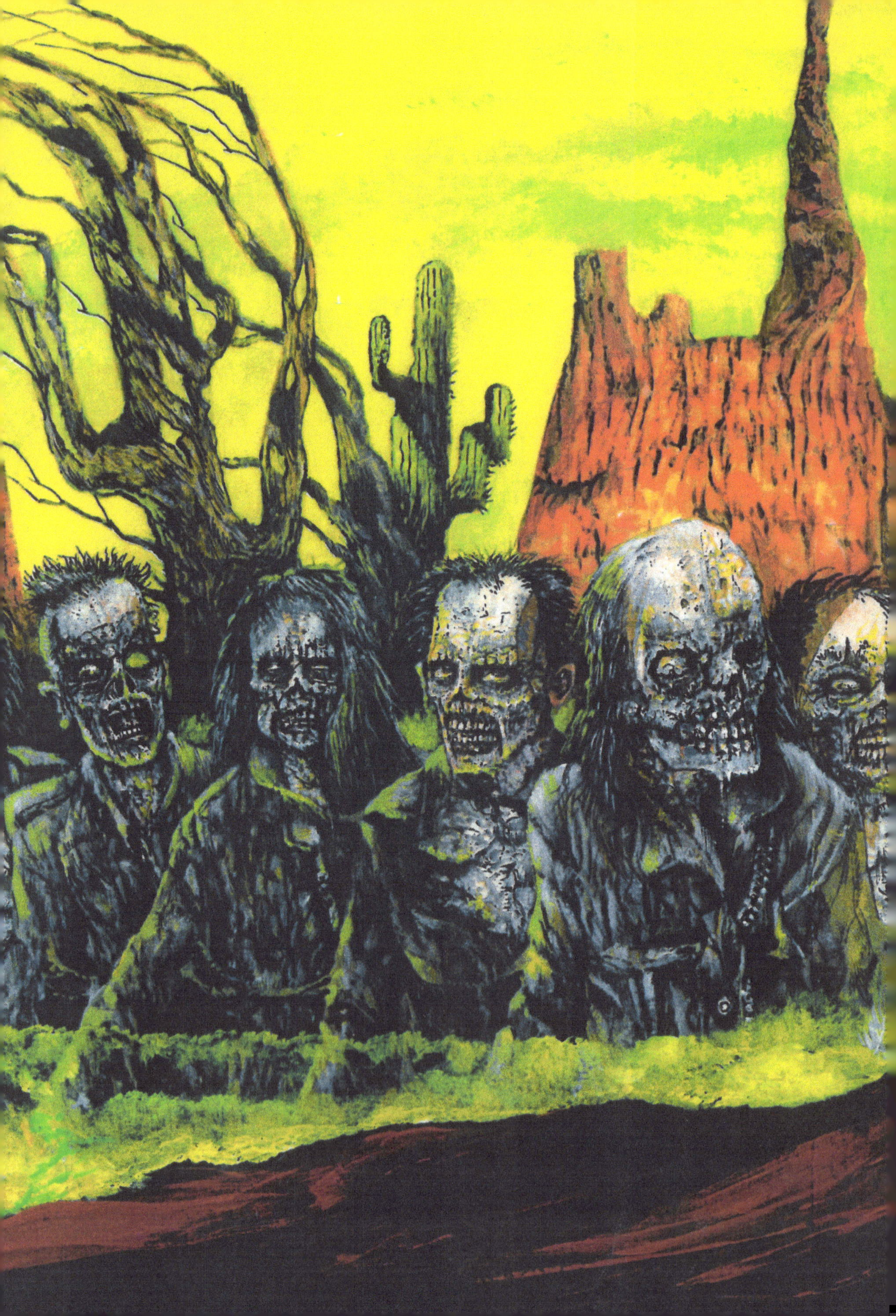

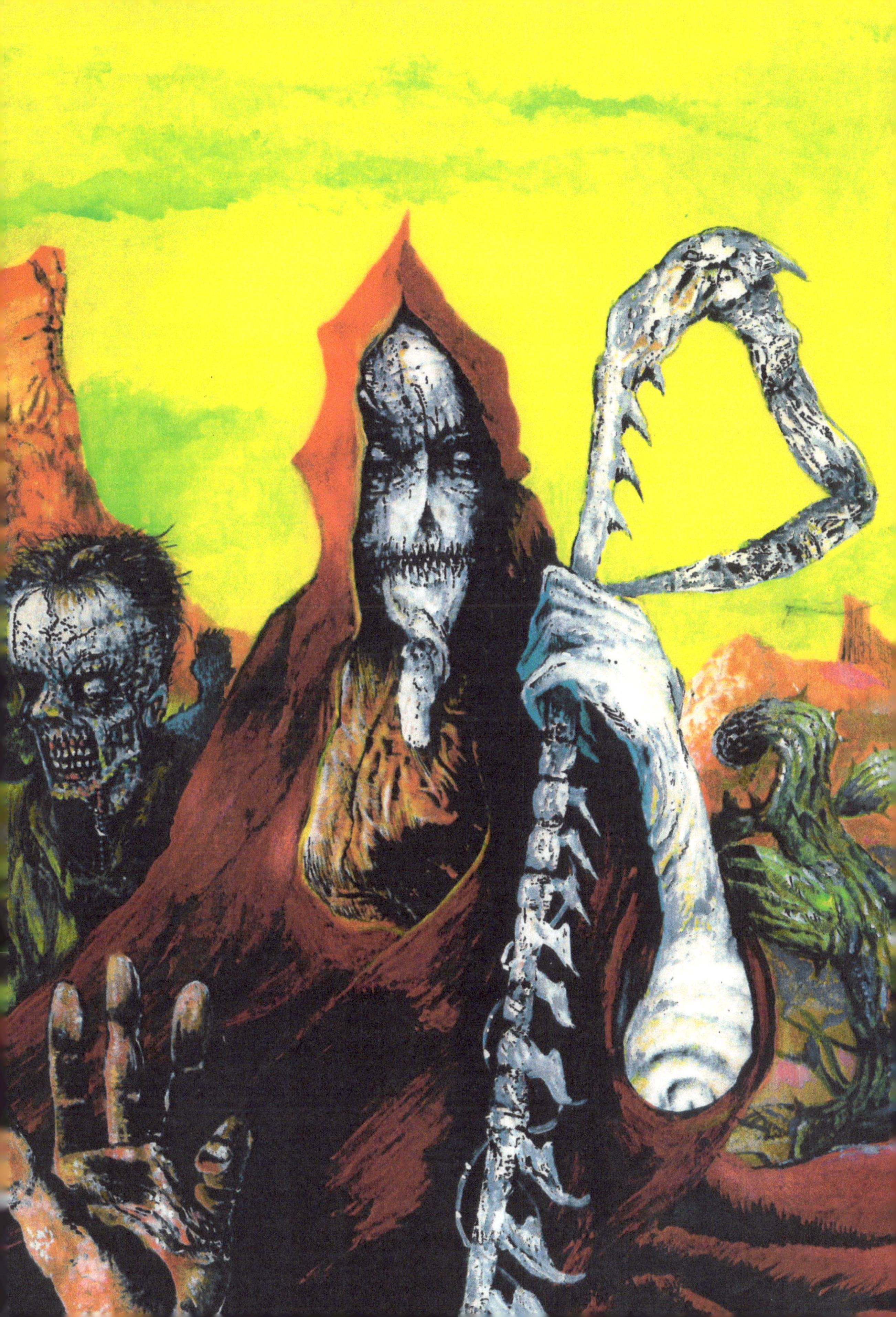

Rigor Mortis

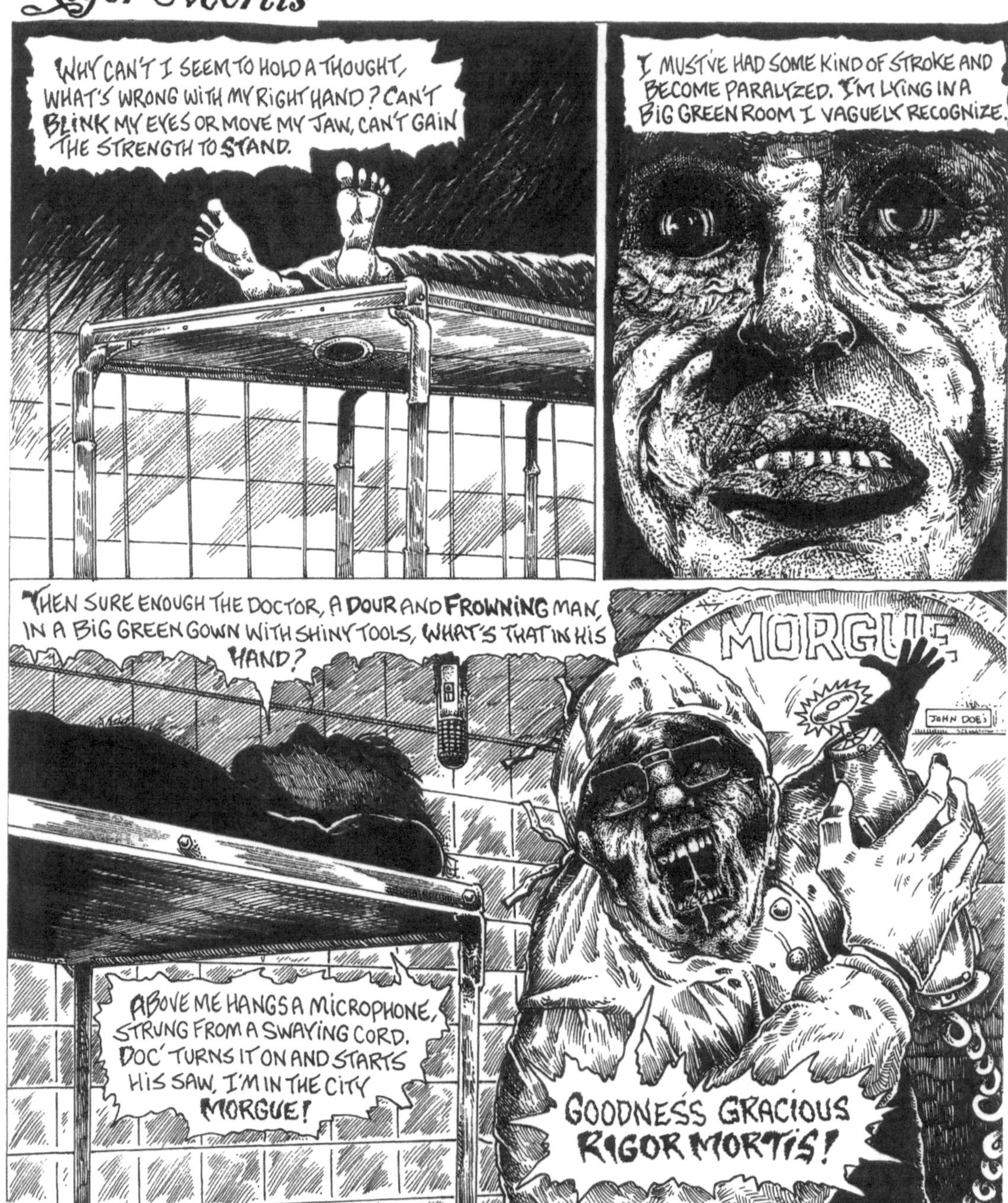

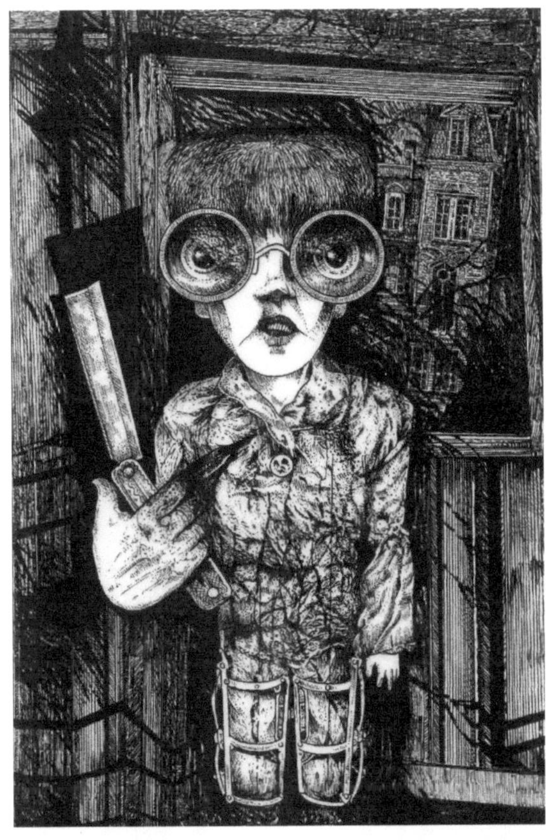
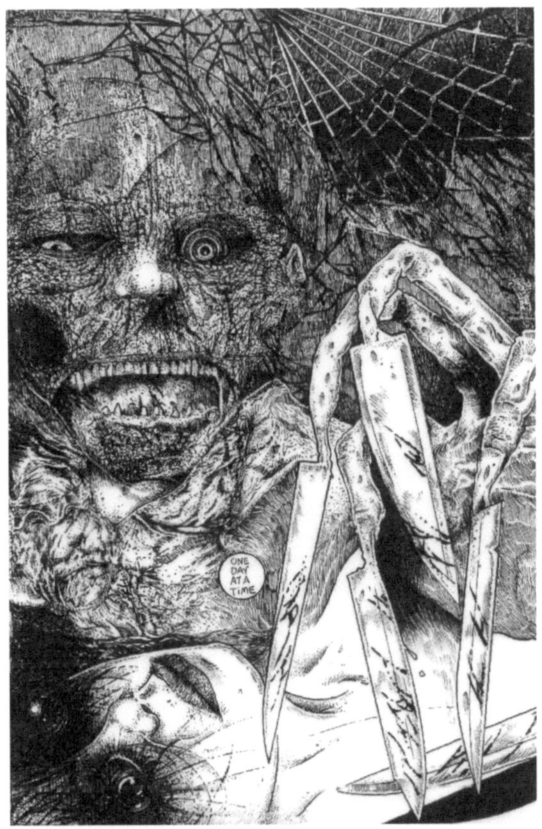
ONE DAY AT A TIME
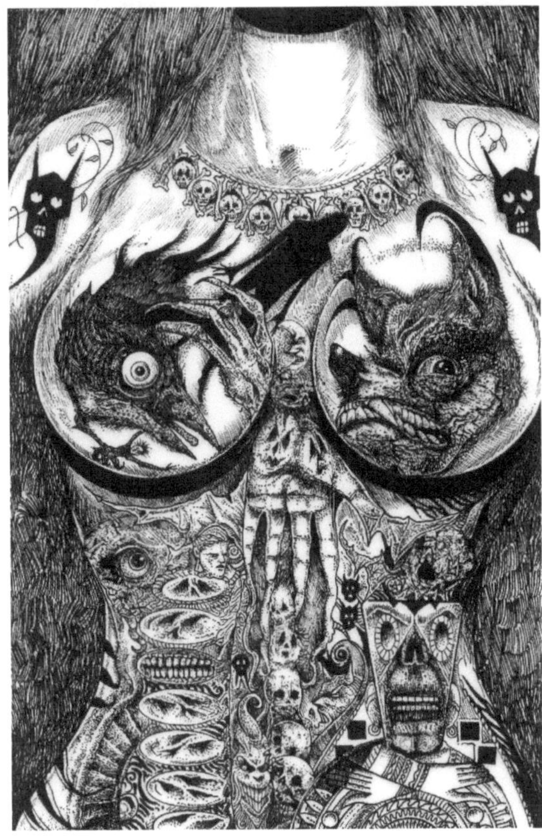
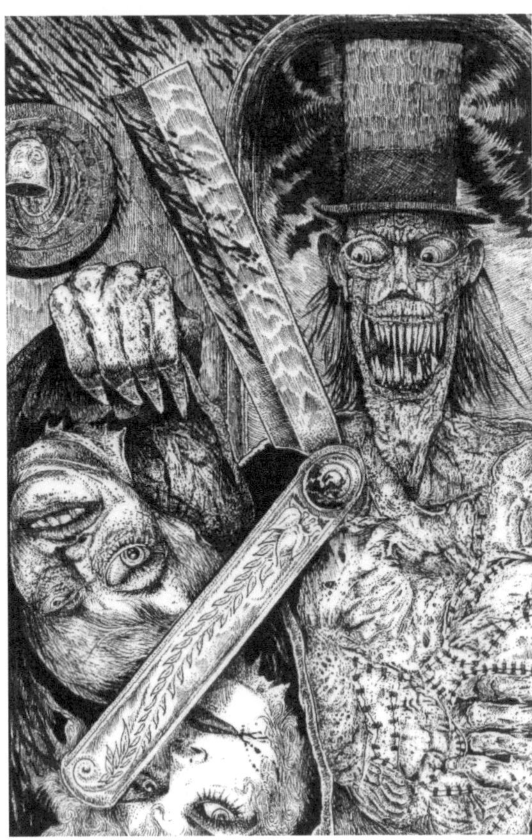

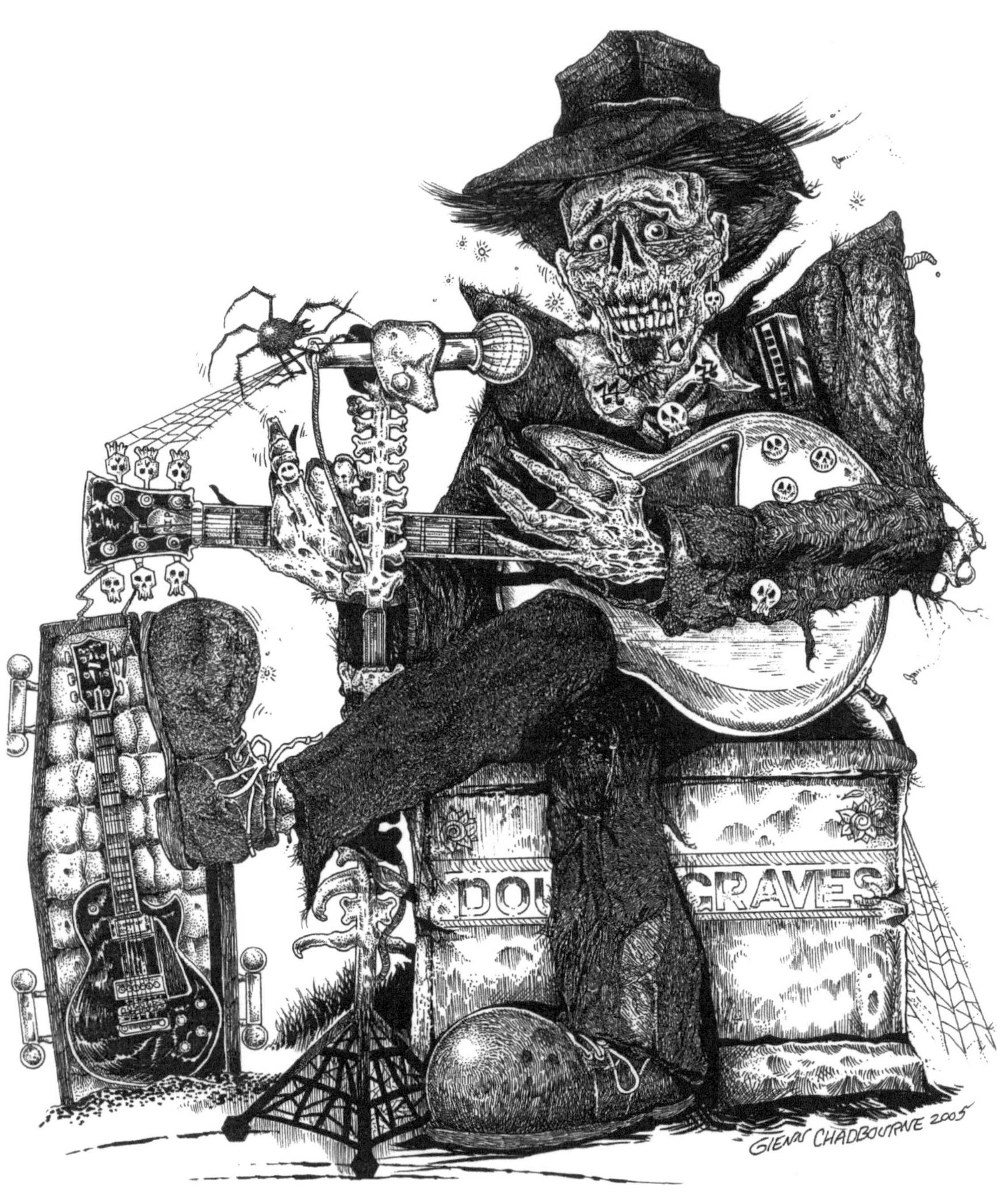
DOU
GRAVES
GLENN CHADBOURNE 2005

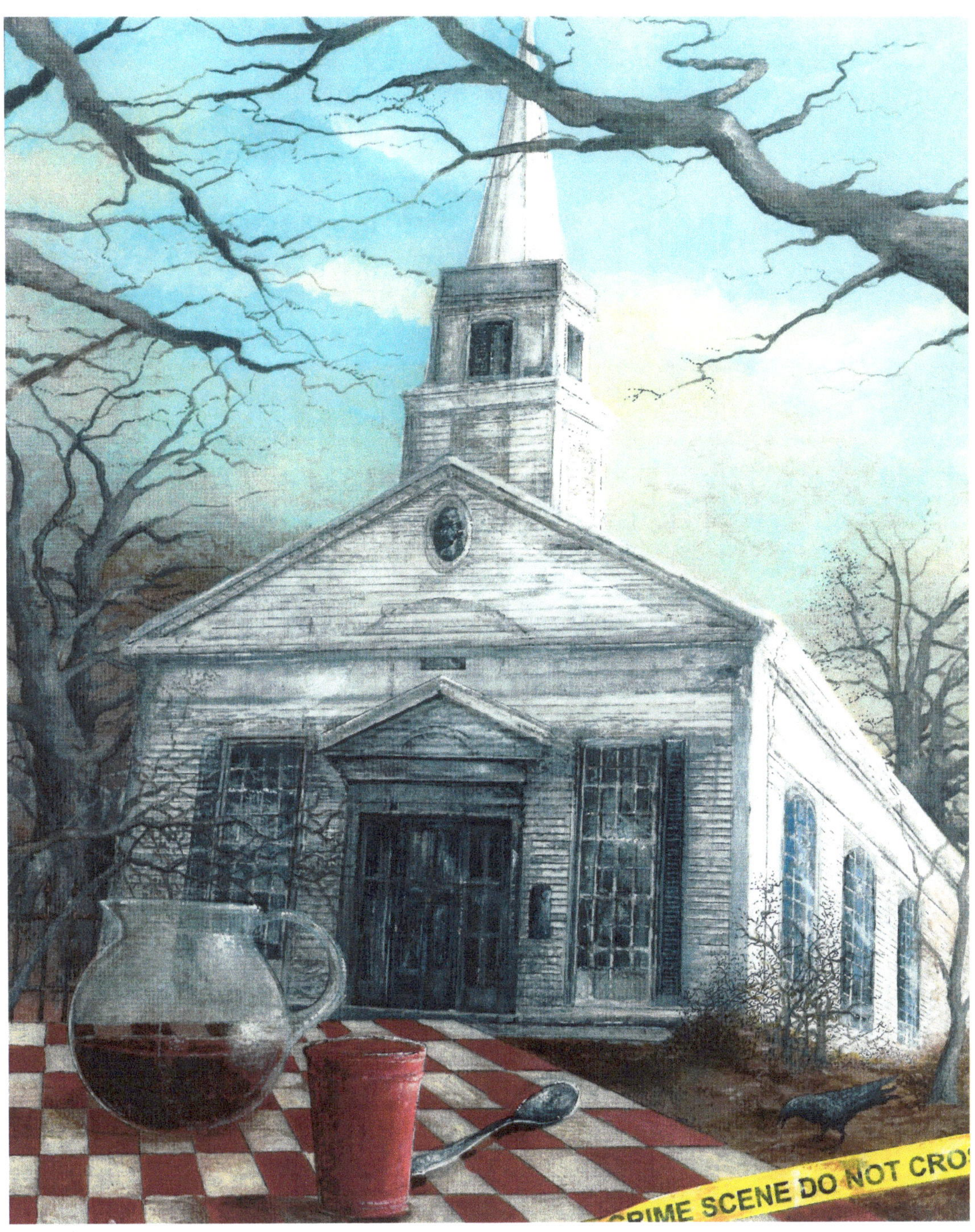
SCENE DO NOT

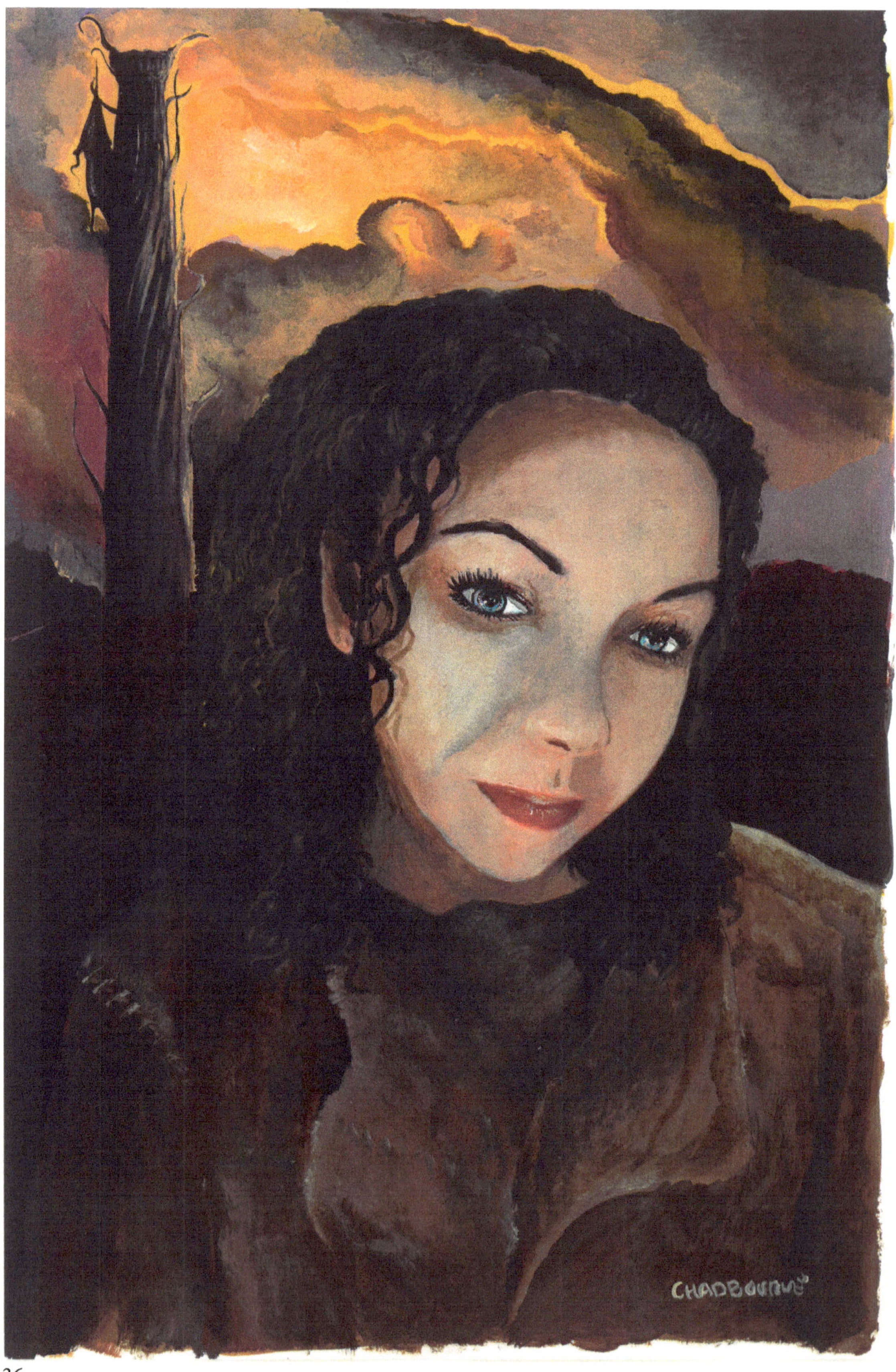
CHADBOURNE

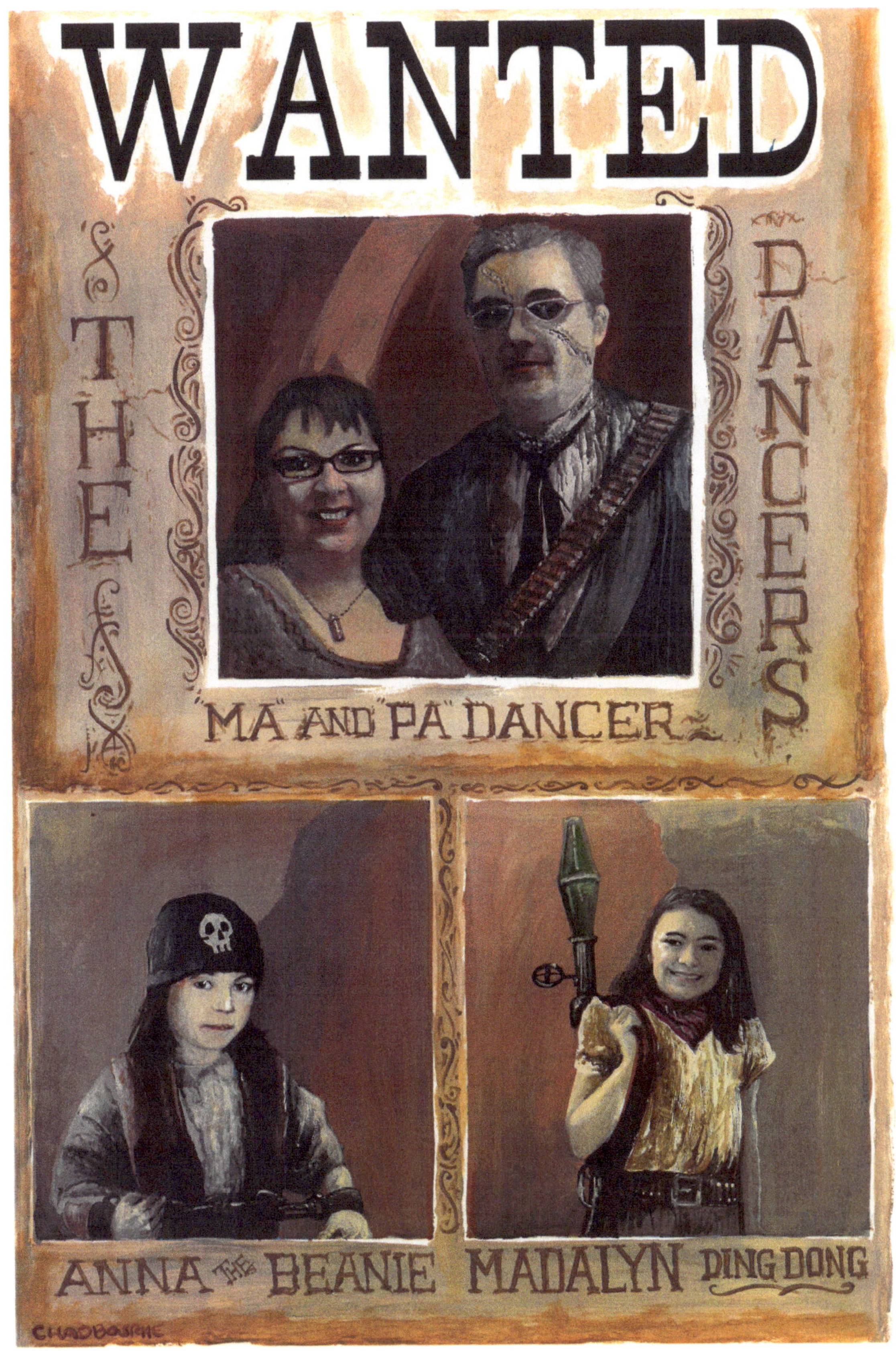
WANTED
THE
DANCERS
"MA" AND "PA" DANCER
ANNA THE BEANIE
MADALYN DING DONG
CHADBOURNE

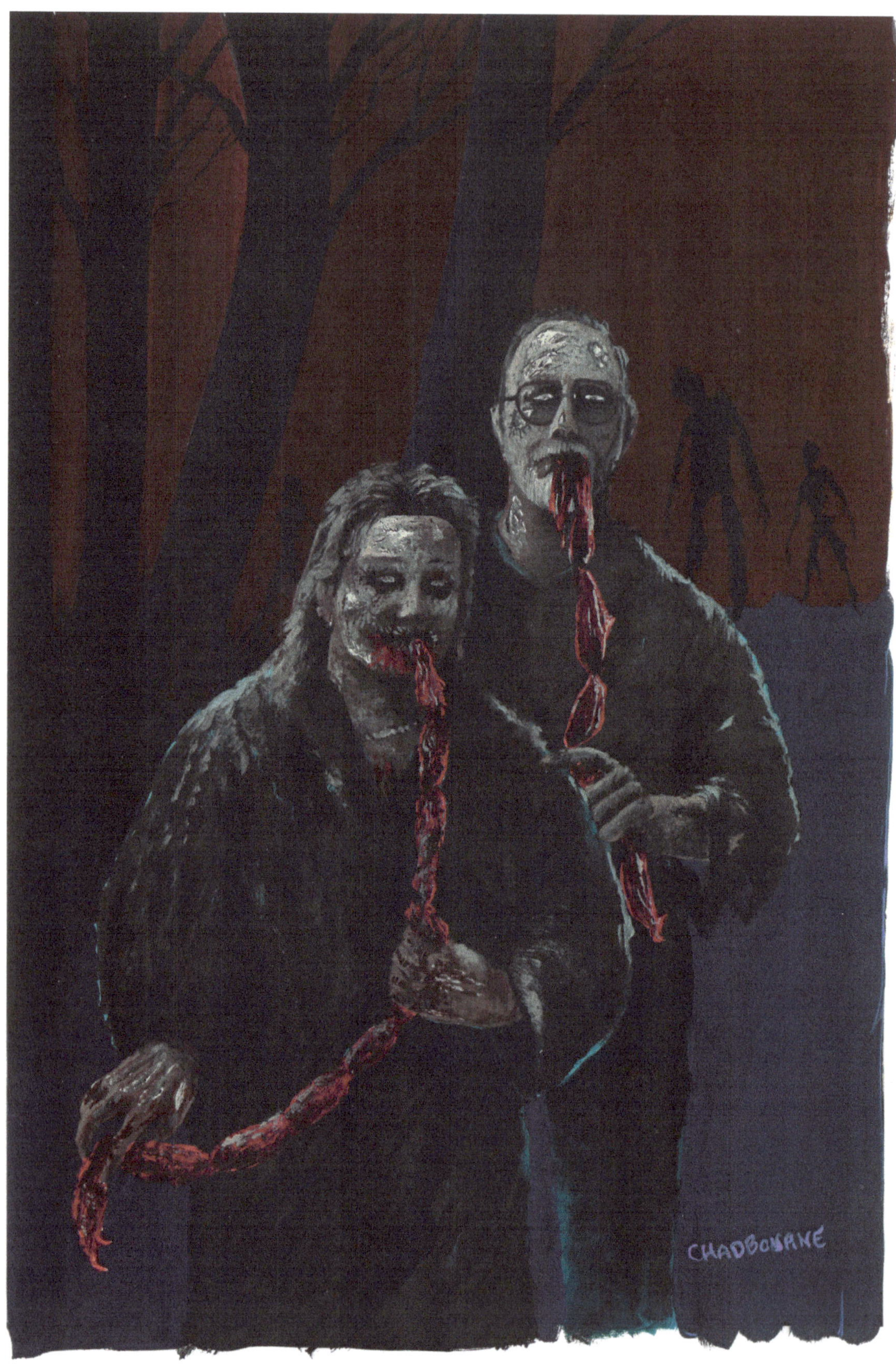

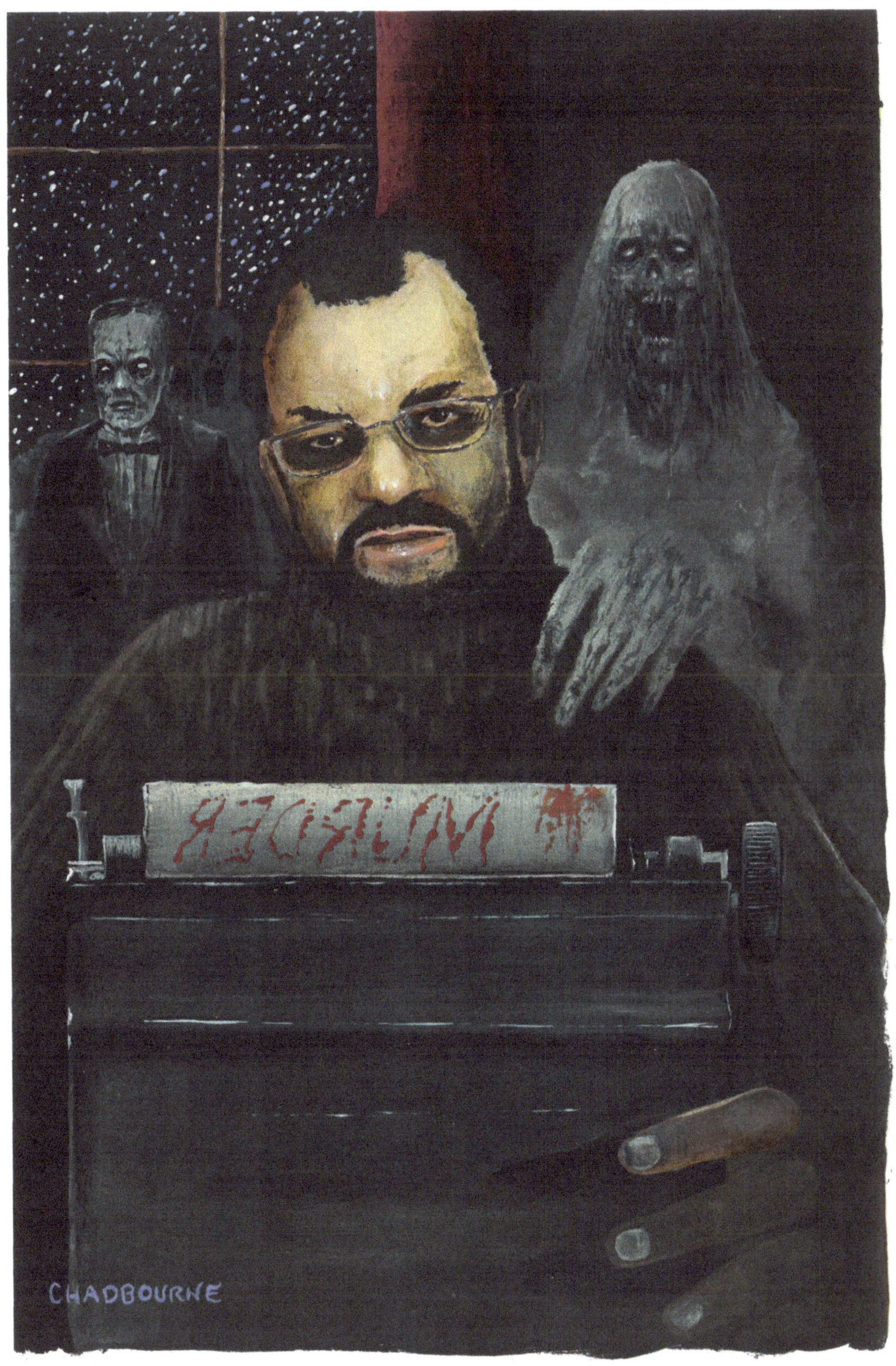
CHADBOURNE

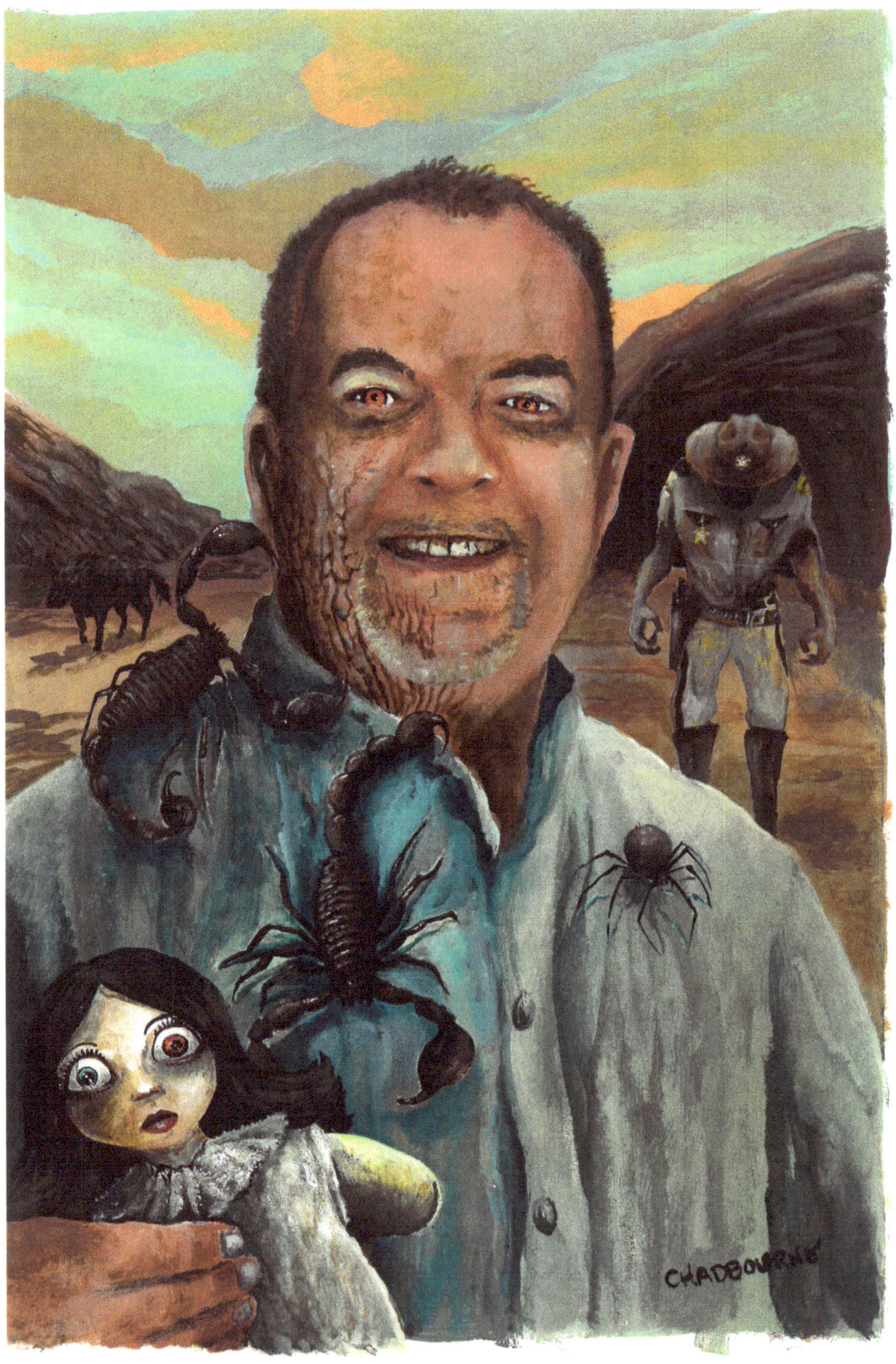
CHADBOURNE

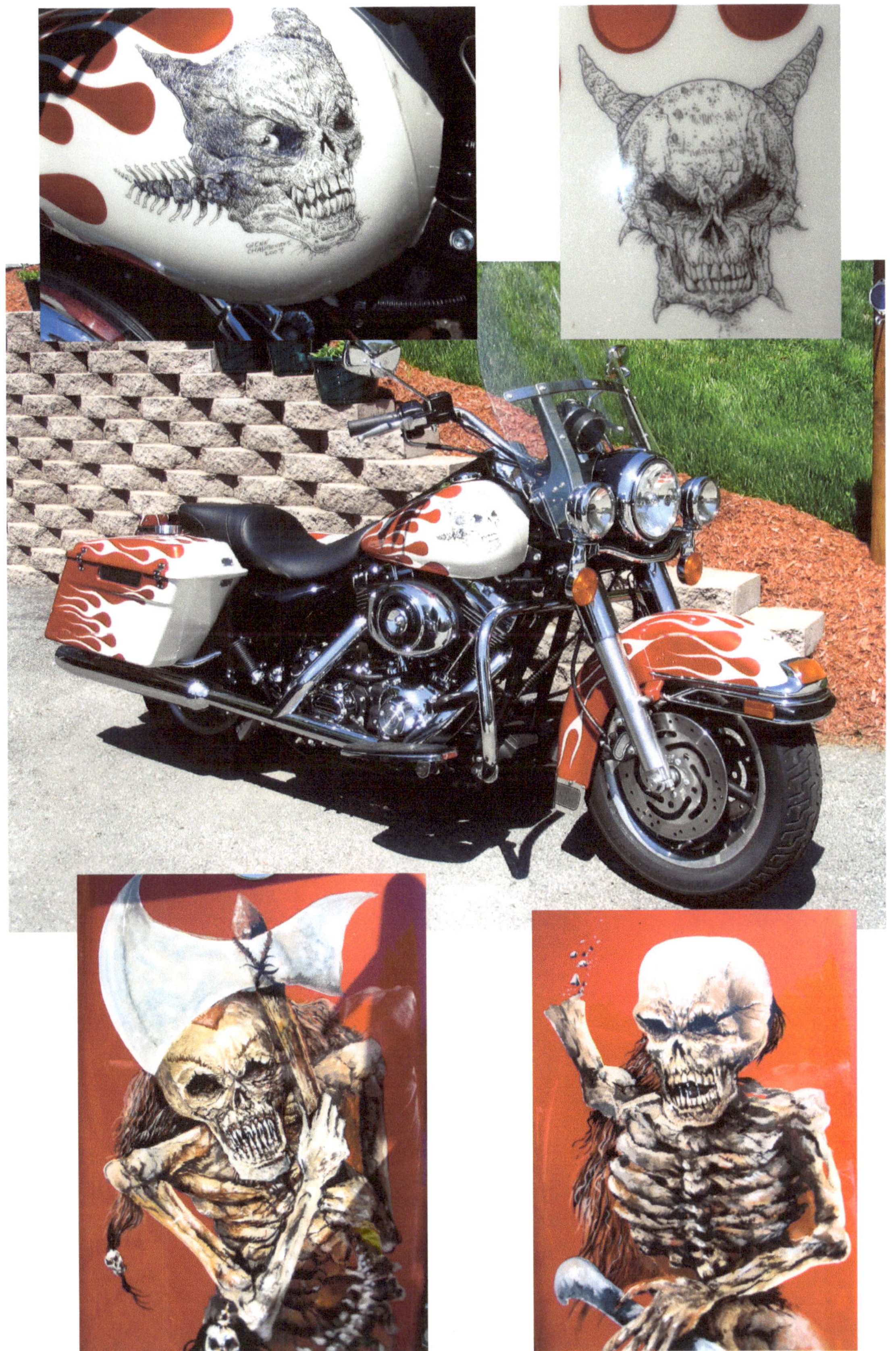

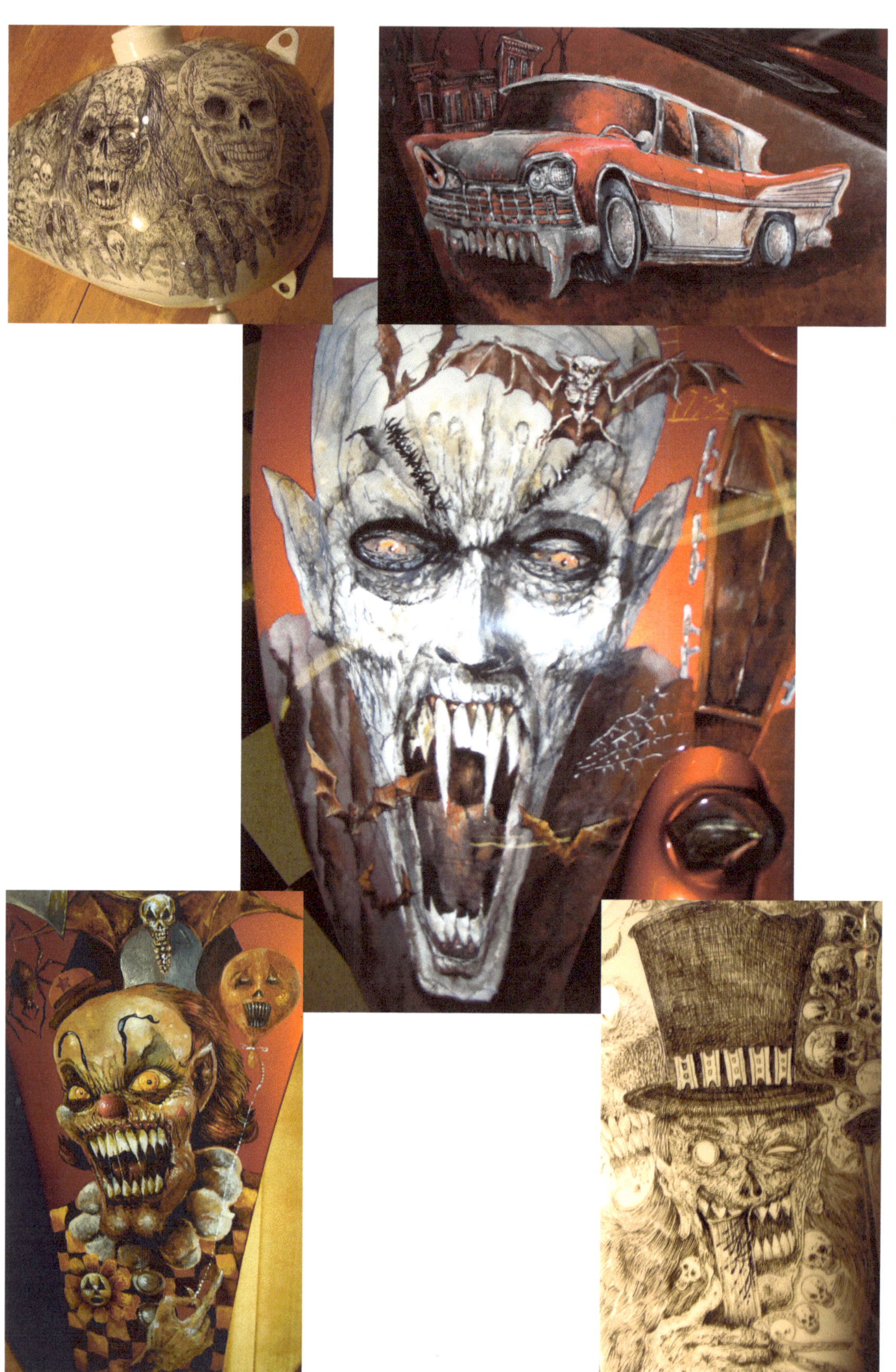

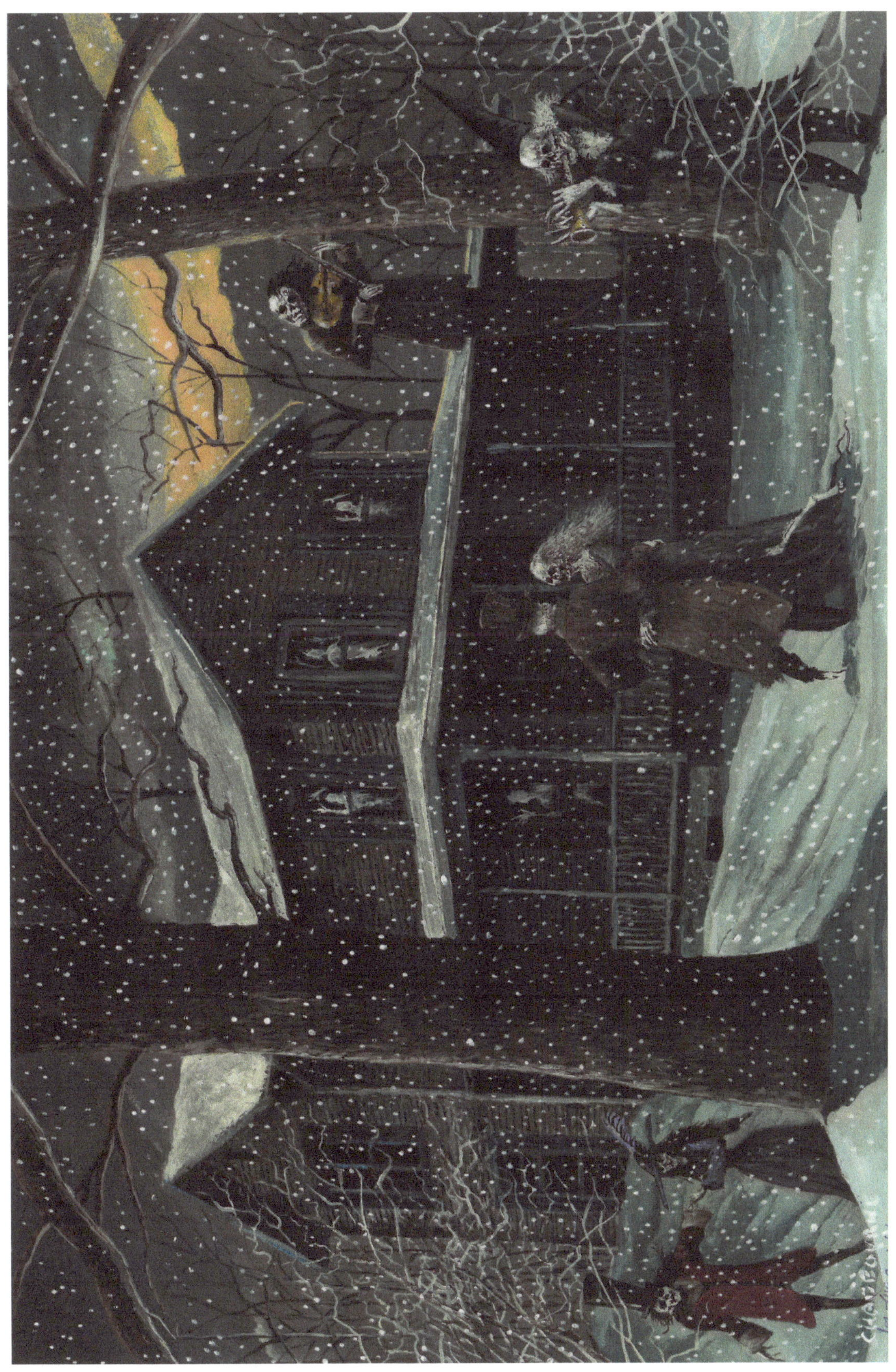

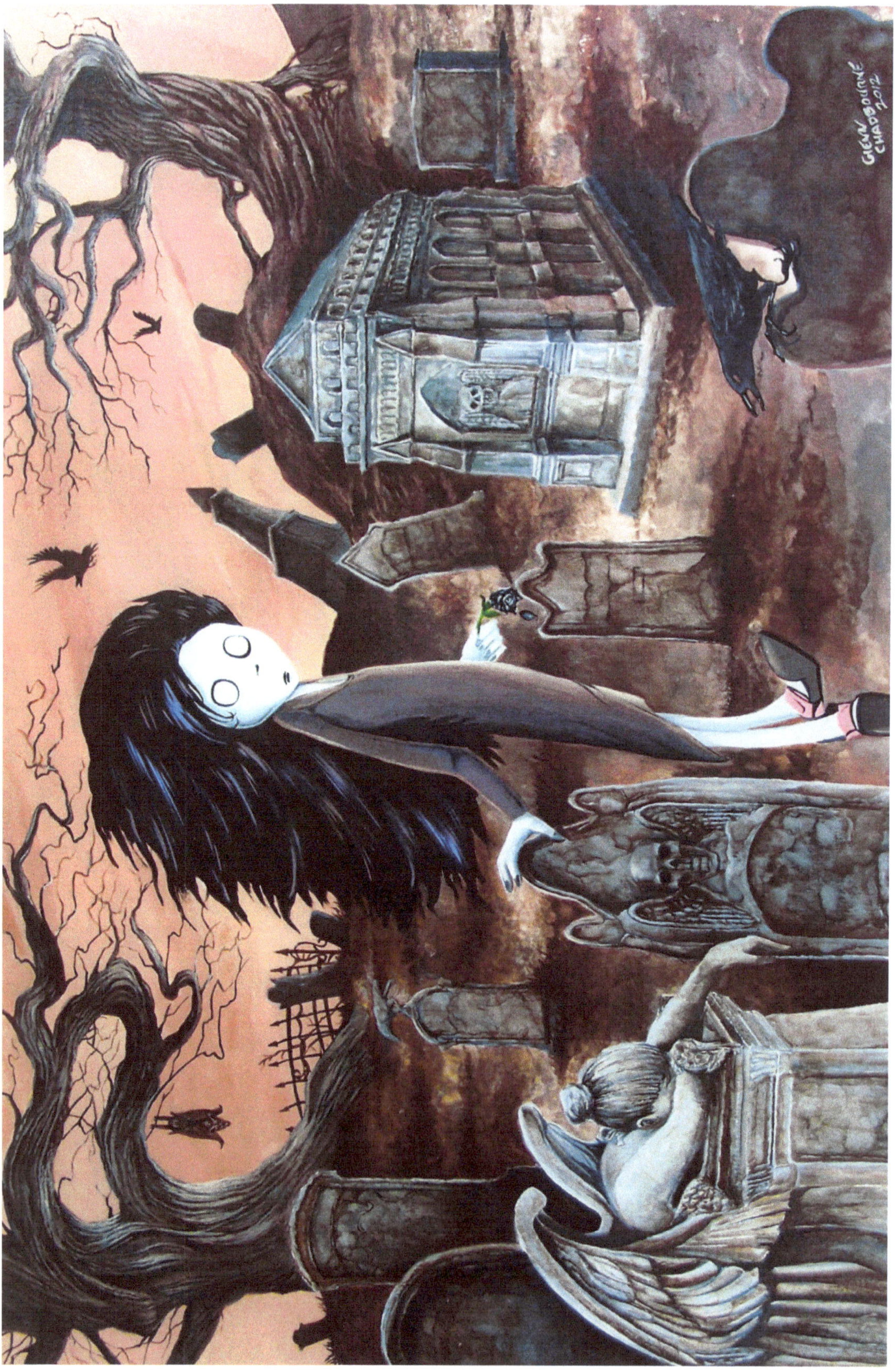
GLENN CHADBOURNE
2012

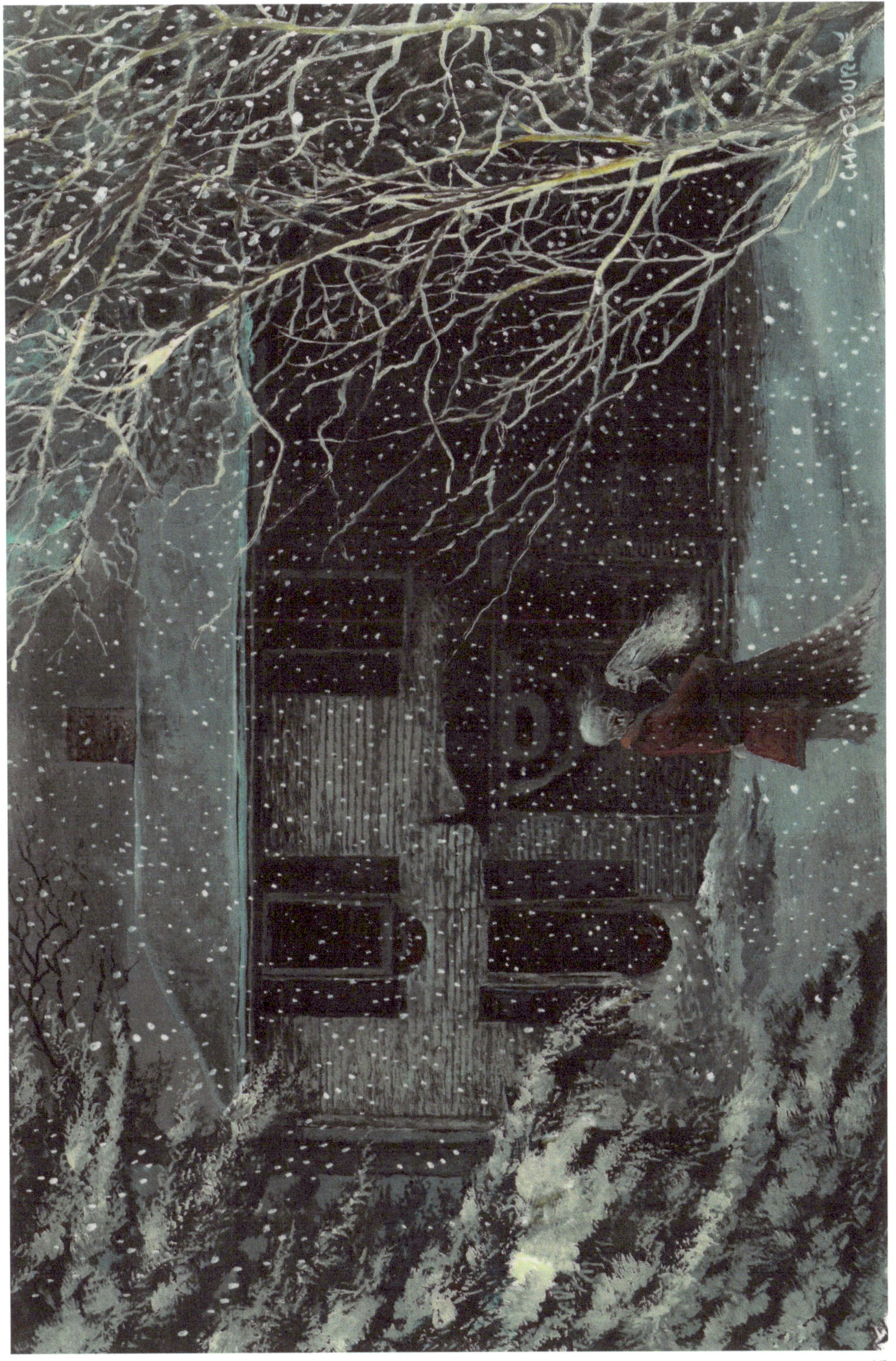

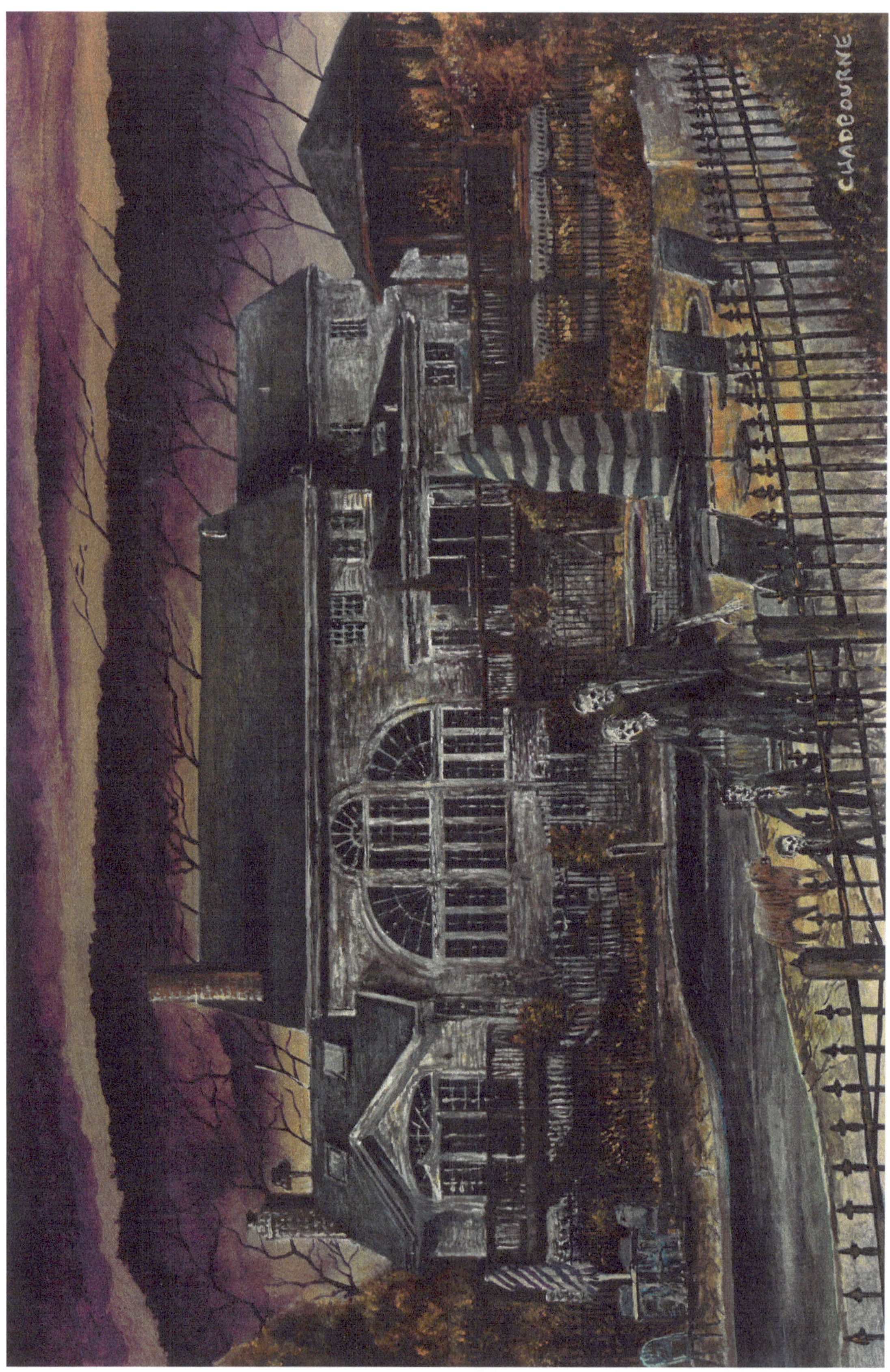
CHADBOURNE

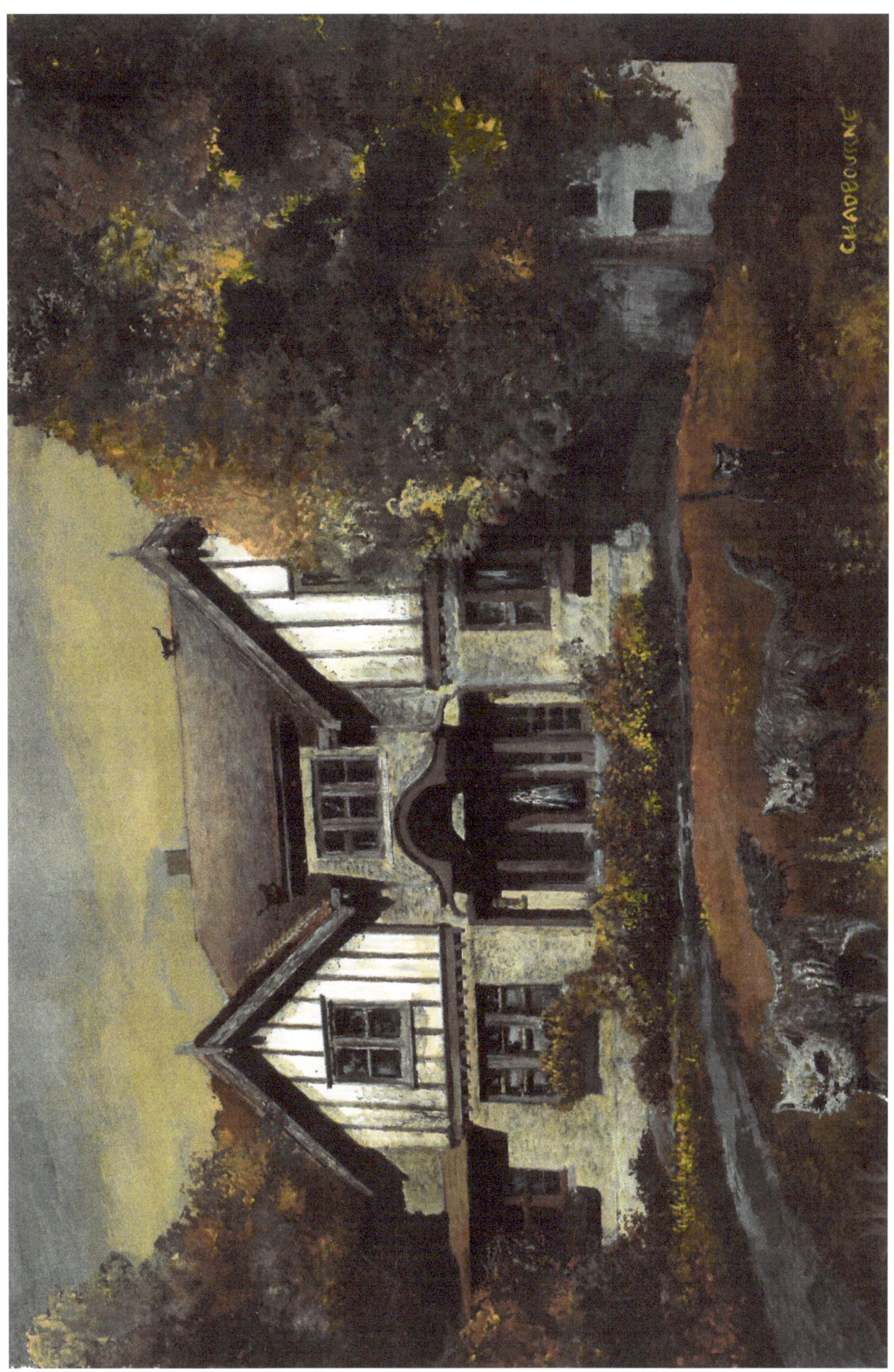
CHADBOURNE

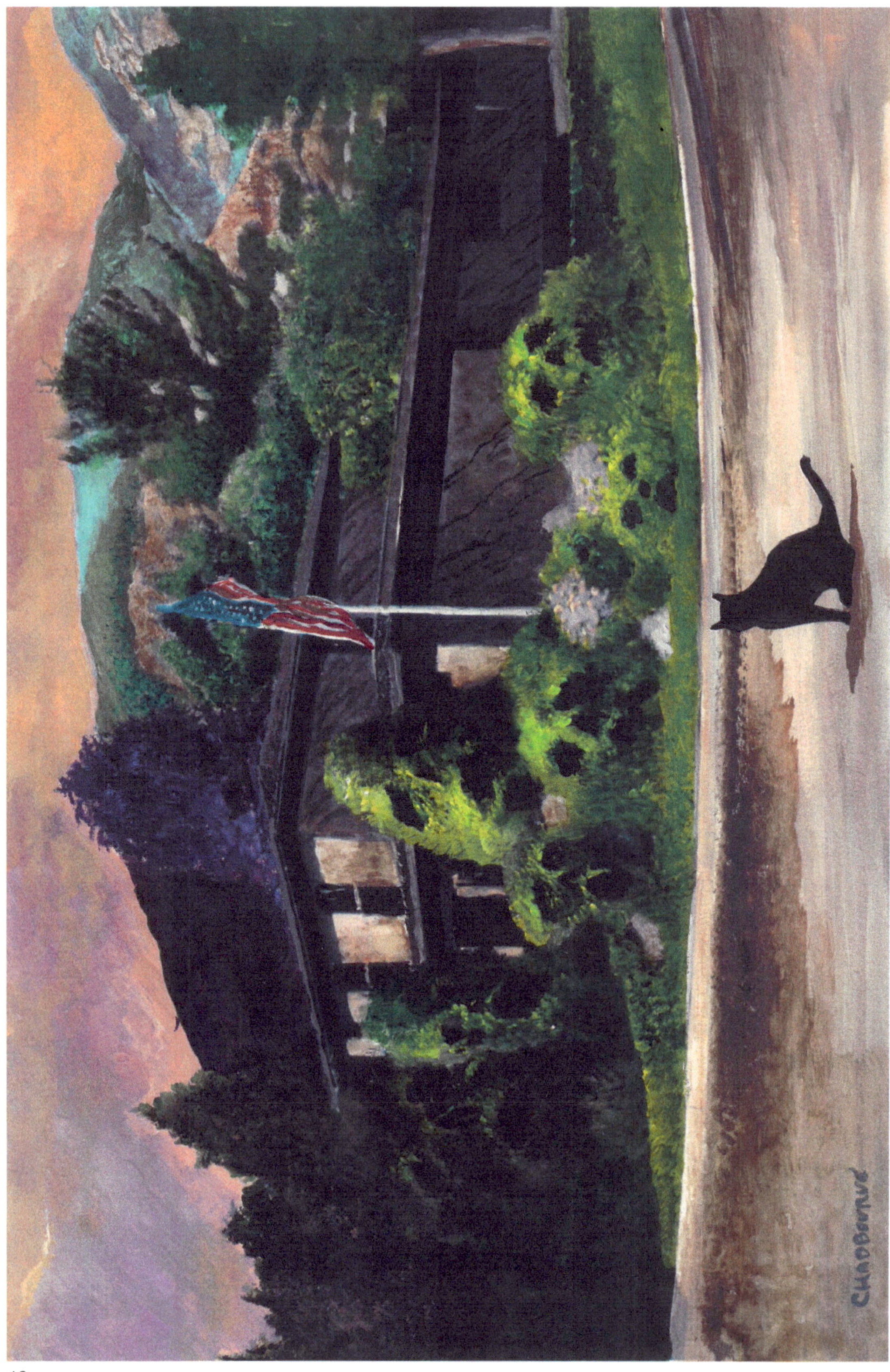
CHADBOURNE

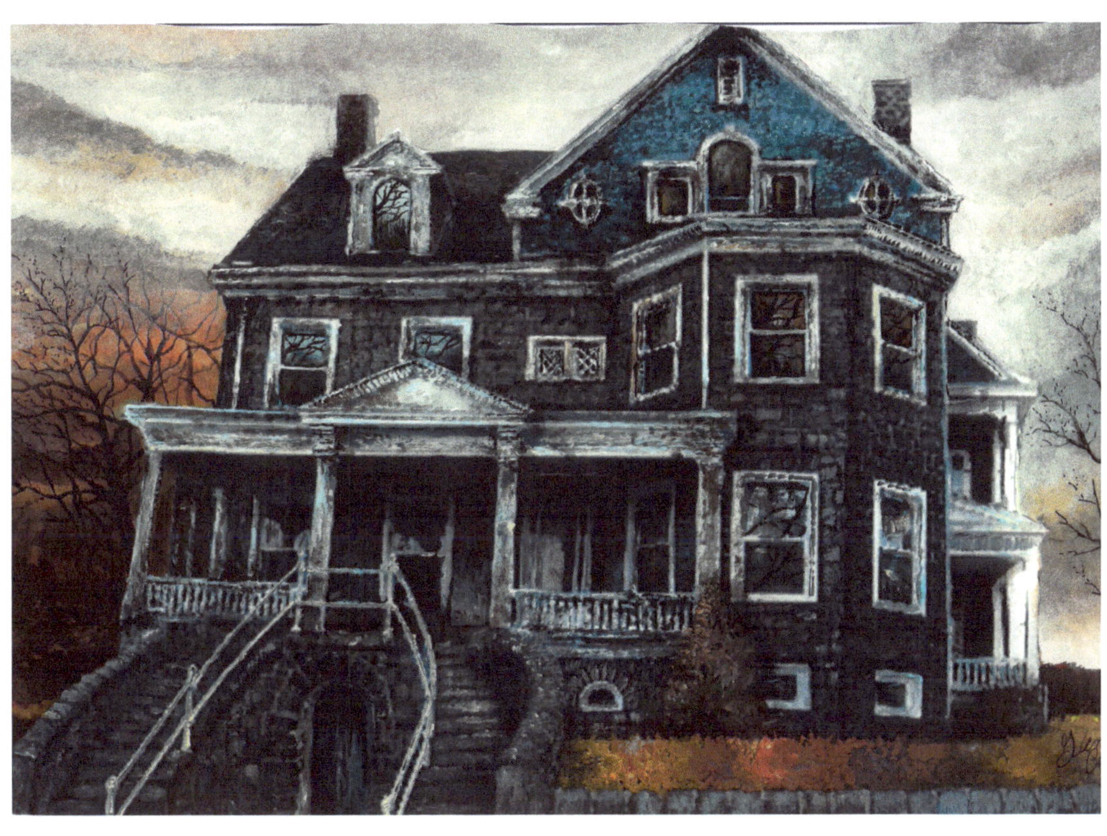

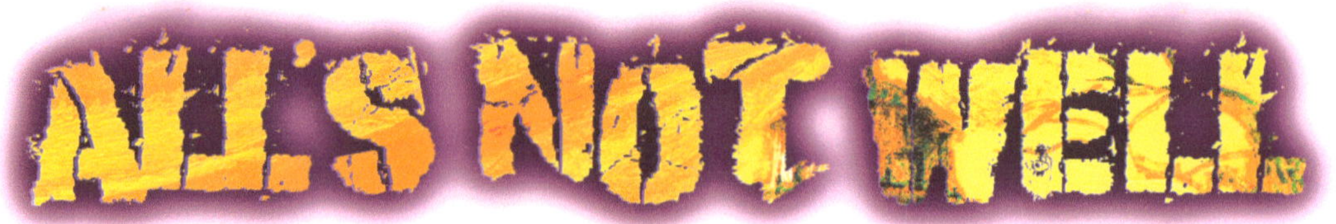

The Gallery of Glenn Chadbourne

Will be published in an oversized hard cover and signed limited edition on Halloween of 2013 by Overlook Connection Press. This massive collection of features almost 300 pages of art, fiction, comics, and a seperate section on Glenn Chadbourne's work with Stephen King fiction.

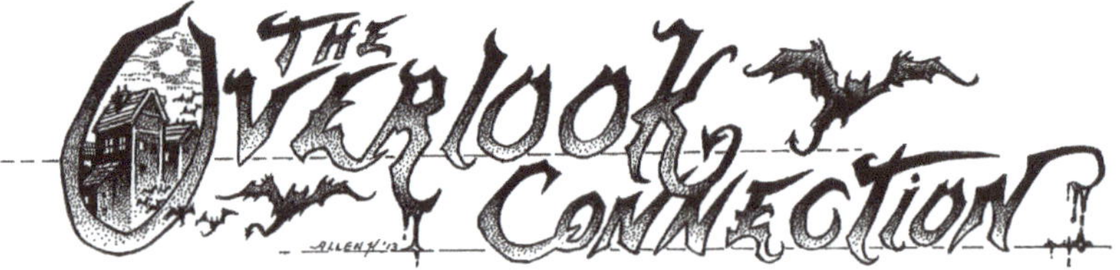

You can find many pieces of original art and reamarqued titles by Glenn Chadbourne by visiting his exclusive sections at **OverlookConnection.com** and **StephenKingCatalog.com**

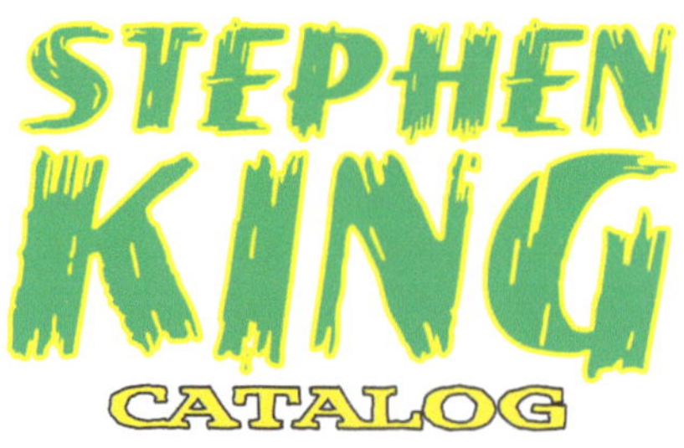

www.ingramcontent.com/pod-product-compliance
Lightning Source LLC
LaVergne TN
LVHW070152110826
845147LV00002B/380
* 9 7 8 1 6 2 3 3 0 0 4 3 2 *